I0639416

Andrew William Hammond

The Poisoned Chalice

A Romantic Drama of American Life in Five Acts

Andrew William Hammond

The Poisoned Chalice
A Romantic Drama of American Life in Five Acts

ISBN/EAN: 9783337021788

Printed in Europe, USA, Canada, Australia, Japan

Cover: Foto ©Andreas Hilbeck / pixelio.de

More available books at **www.hansebooks.com**

THE POISONED CHALICE

A Romantic Drama of American Life.

FOR CLOSET AND STAGE

—— This even-handed justice
Commends the ingredients of our poisoned chalice
To our own lips.—*Shakespeare.*

WASHINGTON, D. C.
THE AUTHOR
1897

THE POISONED CHALICE

A ROMANTIC DRAMA OF AMERICAN LIFE

IN FIVE ACTS

BY
ANDREW WILLIAM HAMMOND

—— This even—
Commends the ingred—
To our own lips —*Sha*

WASHI

THE

DRAMATIS PERSONÆ.

RICHARD FANSHAWE, M. D., a Bohemian.
GEORGE MARLOWE, an artist ; actor in a roving company under the
name of Rugge ; friend of Fanshawe.
COLONEL HERBERT VAUGHN, a country gentleman.
JOHN CARSON, a provincial banker ; friend of Colonel Vaughn.
JUDGE GROTCHET, Colonel Vaughn's lawyer.
JOHN DUNMORE, Nephew of Colonel Vaughn ; law student with
Judge Crotchet ; afterward captain of a slaver.
JONES, Mate of Dunmore's schooner.
GILHOOLY, a waiter ; afterward one of Dunmore's crew.
OLD DAN, Negro slave of Dunmore.

ALIENA DENHAM, a reputed adventuress ; actress in the company
with Marlowe.
ROSE VAUGHN, Daughter of Colonel Vaughn.
MISS BELLE DUNMORE, Cousin of Rose.
Guests of Colonel Vaughn ; Servants ; Hotel Waiters ; Inmates of
a Water Street Dance-house ; Crew of Dunmore's Schooner.
An Octoroon Slave Girl.

Time—1856-'57.

SCENE : ACT I.—The Garden of a Tavern in the Suburbs of an American
Provincial City. ACTS II and III.—Country Residence of Colonel
Vaughn. ACT IV—SCENE I.—Apartments of Marlowe and Fanshawe
in New York. SCENE II.—Interior of a Water Street Dance-house.
ACT V.—Dunmore's Rendezvous on the Coast of Florida.

Between Acts I and II a supposed interval of one month ; between Acts III
and IV, one year ; between Acts IV and V, ten days.

This play is a dramatized version of the author's novel (unpublished) en-
titled " George Marlowe, Artist and Tramp: An Autobiography."

---

(3)

ACT I.

Scene—*The Garden of a Tavern in the outskirts of an American
Provincial City. Landscape, with distant view of woods and
mountains. On left of Scene Veranda of Tavern. Trees, under
which are tables. A* Waiter *in attendance.*

Enter George Marlowe, *poorly dressed.*

Mar., (*glancing round*). I have come too soon, it seems. Miss
Denham has not yet returned. Well, as she must know what
has happened, I must stay until she comes, I suppose—if that
waiter don't turn me out. He seems greatly outraged. [*Laughs.*]
Well, I can't blame him. It is an outrage to come with habili-
ments like these into a place so sacred to store clothes. 'Only
gentlemen admitted.' Well, here is sixpence worth of consola-
tion for him. [*Takes coin from his pocket, steps toward waiter and
then stops.*] No; I can't. With the wolf so near, I must not
part with even a penny. [*Returns coin to pocket, sighs heavily,
and walks thoughtfully up and down.*]

Waiter, (*regarding* Marlowe *suspiciously*). What seedy-look-
ing tramp is that who has althered his moind about givin' me
a cint? Ah, I see who it is. He is one o' them acthorin chaps
from the theayter. That's Misther Rugge, the walkin' gintleman. I didn't recognoise him in his street costume. Begorra,
he's got some cheek to come here in thim cloathes. Maybe he's
got jealous an' come afther the walkin' lady. If he has there'll
be an illegant row betune him an' the foine gintleman that
brings her here. I'll find out, an' if it's the acthress he's afther
I'll tell him something that'll put the foight in him. Hoo,
there'll be a foine shindy.

Enter Fanshawe. *He regards* Marlowe *for a moment, then saunters one side and sits down on the corner of a table.*

Fan. [*Aside:* So, my elusive friend, you are cornered at last,
are you?—if I am not mistaken as to your being the man I
think you are. No, I'm not mistaken. It is George Marlowe and
no one else, but so strangely altered that it is really difficult to

recognize him. Quite down at the heel and out at the elbow, I declare. Romance seems to have been a costly luxury. Love for an actress, I suppose. And now, how am I to approach him—so anxious he seems to shun recognition!]

Waiter, (approaching MARLOWE). What'll yer honor have, sorr?

Mar. Nothing just now. I am only awaiting the arrival of some one who will be here presently.

Waiter. Waitin' the arrival o' some one?

Mar. Yes.

Waiter, (confidentially). It's a lady, isn't it?

[MARLOWE *does not answer. Continues his walk. Waiter follows.*

Waiter. It's a lady, isn't it?

Mar. I don't think it necessary, my friend, that you should know who it is.

Waiter. Oh, mebbe not, sorr. Only I thought yez moight like to have the lady informed that ye're here.

Mar. Ah, true. You are quite right. Yes, it is a lady—Miss Denham, from the theatre; and when she arrives let her know at once, will you, that Mr. Rugge is waiting here to speak with her. [*Gives waiter a coin.*] Don't delay.

Waiter. I'll not, sorr. I'll let her know before she puts her foot out of the carriage door. [*Aside:* Yes, I knew it. It's the acthress he's afther. Hoo! There'll be an illegant row. An' now to rouse the divil o' jealousy that'll put the foight in him.] Yes, sorr; the lady'll arroive prisintly. But, me frind, I'm afther thinkin' that it's not the loikes o' you she'll be wantin' to see.

Mar., (indifferently, continuing his walk). Indeed; and why not?

Waiter. Because she'll be engaged with other company—the other feller, ye know—the gintleman as plays the Count off the stage. He's the boy for her smoiles, an' she's the gal for his money.

Mar., (stopping). What! You insolent hound! Will you go away from me or must I knock you down?

Waiter. Hoo! It's knock me down, is it? That's a different chune, an' it's one that you can't step to, me foine—gintleman.

Mar. Can I not? We shall see. How will this do as a starter for a reel? [*Strikes waiter, who falls back among chairs and tables.*]

Fan. Good! That's my man. That settles his identity.

Waiter, (getting up). Oh, the blaggard! Oh, I'm murthered! Ho, Moike! Denis! Terence! Hans!

. [*Some waiters rush in, followed by some well-dressed loungers.*

FANSHAWE, leaning against table, takes pistol from his pocket.

Waiter. (pointing to MARLOWE). Turn that murtherin' scoundrel out! It's afther killin' me he'd be! He would—so he would.   [*Waiters advance upon* MARLOWE.

Fan., (raising pistol). Hold on there! Stop where you are, or there will be some dead waiters here presently. Verdict of the jury, justifiable homicide. [*Waiters stop and step back.*] So! Now, off with you! [*Rising and replacing pistol. Exeunt waiters.*]

Fan. The scoundrels! But the affair serves my turn most beautifully. It breaks the ice and gives me the opportunity I want. [*Approaches* MARLOWE, *who advances to meet him.*] Sir (*saluting*), am I mistaken in the belief that I address Mr. George Marlowe?

Mar. You are not mistaken, sir; that is my name, though not the one I bear at present. But before I offer any explanation, sir, let me thank you for your interference here in my behalf. You have saved me from being very roughly handled.

Fan. Doubtless; but you need not consider that you owe me any thanks on that account. On the contrary, you might regard me as being indebted to you.

Mar. Indeed, sir! May I know in what way?

Fan. In the opportunity you have given me here for the renewal of a former very agreeable acquaintance. Surely, Mr. Marlowe, it is not possible that you can have forgotten me—Dick Fanshawe. Three years ago, if it is necessary to recall the fact, you and I were frequently together in that circle that gathered round the tables at Pfaff's, in New York.

Mar. No, Mr. Fanshawe, I have not forgotten you. So far from that, sir, I can say that there is no one of that circle of whom I have a more lasting, and I may add a more pleasing, remembrance.

Fan. May I ask, then, why you have so persistently kept out of my way, as it seems to me you have done, since your stay here in town?

Mar. That is a charge, sir, to which I must plead guilty. But let me say that it was not for the reason that a renewal of our former acquaintance would have been in any way displeasing to me. Quite the contrary.

Fan. Well, then, if my curiosity can be excused, may I be so bold as to ask the reason?

Mar. Well, you must consider, Mr. Fanshawe, that our acquaintance at the time you speak of was not such as to permit us to know each other intimately; that soon after it began we separated, and that since that time circumstances have so greatly changed with me that—really, sir—I——

Fan. Oh, spare yourself the explanation. Perhaps I can understand reasons that you hesitate to give. You have been hard pressed by misfortune since the time we speak of.

Mar. Quite true, sir.

Fan. And not having any reason to suppose that I was unlike the rest of the world, that keeps out of a man's way when Fortune deserts him, you have kept out of mine through fear that you might meet a rebuff—that I might not wish to renew acquaintance with one in disgrace with Fortune and men's eyes.

Mar. Well, sir, I must confess to having had some such thoughts, but I see now that I was mistaken; that I ought to have known better, and I beg your pardon most sincerely.

Fan. Oh, let it pass. It was not complimentary; but in view of the human nature that underlies it, it is easily overlooked. You gentlemen of the artistic mould are such supersensitive spirits—you shrink from even the suspicion of a slight. So, with this regard, we will say nothing more about it, and if it is agreeable to you, take a new hold of the old acquaintance. [*Offers his hand.*]

Mar. With all my heart. [*Taking* FANSHAWE's *hand.*] Nothing in the world could give me greater pleasure.

Fan. And a hold that shall stand the test of ill fortune—and of good fortune, too, I hope. And now, that we are once more on the old familiar footing, let us sit down here and have a julep and a talk over old times. [*They sit down at a table under a tree in front.*]

Enter the WAITER, *with glasses and a pitcher, which he places on the table. He has a badly bruised eye from the blow received from* MARLOWE.

Fan., (to waiter). So, Mr. Gilhooly, is it there ye are once more? Sure, it's a foine oye ye have intirely.

Waiter. Is it, sorr? Sure, an' I'm willin' to give one to yer honor if yez consider it ornamintal. [*Exit.*

Fan., (*filling glasses*). Well, here is to the memories of the
past and the hopes of the future. [*They drink.*] But before we
come to tender memories, there is a matter upon which I would
like some information. How is it that I find you here, an actor
in a roving company? Three years ago I left you a rising artist
in New York.

Mar. You find me here for the reason that three years ago I
ceased to be a rising artist. Not having any money—having
failed to be wise in the day of success—I was obliged to take to
some other means of earning a living, which I did by taking to
the stage and joining a strolling company. It is the old story.
You know how popular the dramatic profession is with people
who have failed in life.

Fan. Yes, it seems to be. But there is a mystery still unex-
plained. I can't understand how an artist of your ability should
fail to win success anywhere.

Mar. That has also a simple explanation. It was due to a
discovery I made one day that my success as an artist was not
due to the merit of my work, but that it was altogether due to
the criticism, or rather the lavish praise, given to my pictures
by a couple of art critics of my acquaintance, presumed friends
of mine.

Fan. Oh, indeed!

Mar. Yes; and it was a discovery so disheartening, one that
hurt my pride, or perhaps my vanity, so much that I made an
attempt to convince myself that it was not true. So I hid myself away from the critics, and for a year or so painted in obscurity, sending my work out under the assumed name of Rugge.
Well, the result was only to confirm the truth of the discovery.
I never sold a picture from the day I took leave of the critics.
I was then obliged to confess to the heart-breaking truth—that
my success as an artist had not been due to merit, but was purely
the result of newspaper laudation.

Fan. H'm! You are not the first artist who has made that
discovery, I'm thinking. But did you not allow your friends,
the critics, to take you up again?

Mar. I was quite willing that they should do so, so strong
was the persuasion of an empty pocket; but in the meantime
something had happened. It had been discovered that the
critics I mention had taken money from artists whose work

would not justify the laudation these critics had given them, and they had been discharged from their newspapers. In fact, I had myself unsuspectingly lent money among them.

Fan. Which, it is not necessary to say, had not been repaid?

Mar. Not a penny of it. Well, I struggled on for a year longer, earning a precarious living by painting for the auction-rooms, and then, just as I was on the verge of actual starvation, a friend of mine, a theatrical man, learning of my condition, offered me a position in his company. I accepted. In due time we took the road; and here I am, a stranded actor. And so ends my story.

Fan. And a sad one it is, truly. [*Aside:* So, then, it was not love for an actress that turned him into a stroller. So much the better for the object I have in view.] But stranded actor, you say? What! Has it come to this with you?

Mar. It has. Bad luck and empty benches, resulting partly from competition with a minstrel show here in town, have brought us to the usual fate—break up and a midnight exit from the stage door.

Fan. In which the walking gentleman don't seem to have participated!

Mar. That is for the reason that, as walking gentleman, I want an exit more in keeping with my line of parts. I am in debt for a board bill. I have not yet acquired the art of walking away from that gracefully. Besides, there's my stage ward-robe——

Fan. Surely, you are in a bad plight. And now, if you will permit the question, may I ask what you intend to do?

Mar. Hunt up employment of some kind—something in the artistic line, if it can be had. The search for it is one of the objects that has brought me here.

Fan. This is hardly the locality in which to find it. Nose-painting is the only artistic work done on these premises. Fine specimens on exhibition daily. [*This to the listening loungers, who take the hint and walk off.*] Nevertheless, I think something in the line you want can be found if you will permit me to do a friend's office and obtain it for you.

Mar. Willingly. And I don't mind saying that I am at so low an ebb that I could accept a job at whitewashing, if nothing better offered.

2

Fan. Something better will offer. I have in mind something that I think would suit you. How would you like the position of drawing master in a gentleman's family?

Mar. It is not a question of liking, my dear friend. Beggars must not be choosers.

Fan. Well, it so happens that I know where a drawing master is wanted. It is in a gentleman's family, living a few miles in the country. And I can say that you are already known there by reputation. One of your pictures is in possession of the family, and the master of the house values it so highly that he has more than once spoken to me about what he calls the mysterious disappearance of the artist.

Mar. Let him but say the word and the artist shall reappear.

Fan. That word shall be said tomorrow. [*Aside:* And now for the first step toward the grand object I am aiming at.] I suppose, my friend, that you have not given up ambition—that the hope of eventually winning recognition and success as an artist is very dear to you.

Mar. So much so, my dear friend, that there is scarcely any sacrifice I would not make to bring that hope to fruition.

Fan. Good! I find thee apt. Would you regard marriage, then, as too great a sacrifice to be made with that object in view?

Mar. Marriage?

Fan. Yes. With a young lady, say, who was very rich, while you were very poor!

Mar. I don't think I should regard that as much of a sacrifice at the present state of my fortunes. I confess there was a time when I would have done so, but such romance has quite vanished with me. Do you see these holes? [*Pointing to the holes in his coat.*] That is where it went out.

Fan. Well said, my lad. And that is where wisdom went in. Contact with the sharp corners of the world, if it makes holes in one's coat, lets the romance out of the best of us.

Mar. It has let the romance out of me, and something has kept it company that I would much rather not have parted with. [*Sighs.*] Not forever sweet are the uses of adversity.

Fan. Oh, cheer up. You are so much the better fitted for the life of this world. We must be wise, yield to life's hard conditions and make the best of them. Such is my creed.

Mar. I can find it easy to accept it for mine. And now, as to this marriage you speak of.

Fan. Well, in the family where I shall introduce you as drawing master is a young lady, the daughter of the house, who is heiress to millions. She will be your pupil. She is very beautiful and romantic withal, and I can foresee that when she has heard your story and knows you for what you are, she will fall in love with you and you can marry her. Then, with fortune and position yours, the artistic recognition you covet is within your reach. Remember, my friend, that you are in a country where merit such as yours must buy its way to recognition or—emigrate.

Mar. Well, really, my dear friend—what shall I say? In some respects—but to enter an honorable family with such an object in view——   .

Fan. Would not be the part of an honorable man, you would say? True; I knew you would think so, and it was the answer I expected. Now, hear me further. There are circumstances connected with such a part that quite redeem it from anything dishonorable, but, on the contrary, impart to it an element of chivalry and romance. In marrying the young lady you would save her from a terrible fate.

Mar. Indeed!

Fan. Yes; or what I regard as such. The young lady is sought in marriage by a man who is unworthy of her, and who, if he succeeds in marrying her—and there is great danger that he will do so—will wreck her happiness forever. It is a fate from which I would save my fair cousin Rose, as I would save a dear sister.

Mar. Your cousin?

Fan. Yes; but that part has been changed. She is now the sister to me.

Mar. Oh, I see.

Fan. Yes; and naturally I feel some interest in her welfare; and I will further confess that the hope of saving her from this man is the great object I have in view in placing you in her father's house. Now, you understand me? Will you undertake the part?

Mar., (*after a moment's reflection*). I will. [*They shake hands.*] I will woo the young lady and save her from the villain—if I can.

Fan. I can't say the man is a villain. As men go, he might be considered an honorable man, but secretly he leads a life that would wreck the happiness of any woman he might marry. He is prominent in social life here. He is the banker Carson.

Mar. I have heard of him. And the name of the young lady?

Fan. Is Miss Rose Vaughn.

Mar. Is she the daughter of Colonel Vaughn?

Fan. She is. Do you know the Colonel?

Mar. I have a partial acquaintance with him—made behind the scenes of the theatre here. He only knows me, however, as Rugge, the actor—to call me one.

Fan. He will soon know you in your true character—and much sooner than I expected—for here he comes.

Enter COLONEL VAUGHN, *escorting* MISS DENHAM. *Engaged in conversation, they cross the stage and go out at one of the exits.*

Fan. The Colonel seems greatly taken with your leading lady. I have noticed that every night of her engagement he has occupied a private box at the theatre, and that every day he comes here to take her out for a drive. And that leads me to ask a question concerning her. She is very beautiful. Is she a good woman as well?

Mar. I have no reason in the world for thinking otherwise.

Fan. Then perhaps a word of warning might not be thrown away upon her.

Mar. A word of warning! Of what nature?

Fan. Well, Colonel Vaughn, although a very honorable man in other respects, is not very scrupulous as regards women. He is very rich, and, besides, has personal qualities that make him dangerous. A word of warning now might save some unhappiness hereafter.

Mar. I don't think the lady will need it. On the contrary, the Colonel might need a word of warning himself. She is not a woman to be trifled with. Beauty is not her only charm. She has intellect, education, and a strong will. Besides, she has a fascination more potent still. She is difficult to read. Upon my life I can't make out whether she is a woman of really noble character or a superior kind of adventuress.

Fan. A woman not to be trifled with, I should say. But the question arises, What has made such a woman an actress in a roving company?

Mar. The fascination of the stage, doubtless. It is a very potent lure, you know, for brilliant and beautiful women—on the hither side of the footlights.

Fan. Yes, and a fatal one in most cases. Brilliant moths of that kind lie thick around those candles. And very badly scorched—some of them. Well, I wish the Colonel would come in. I am impatient to let him know that the painter of the picture he values so highly will become the drawing master he is in search of.

Mar. And while we are waiting, suppose you tell me something about yourself. Why is it that I find you in this provincial town? I was greatly surprised to see you across the footlights.

Fan. The town is my native home. I am practicing medicine here—if a doctor can be said to do that who has no patients. When I finished my hospital probation in New York I came home to practice. I didn't find it, and so fell back on my former trade of novel writing. My work I sell to local publishers, and what with this and what with an occasional check from my dad, I manage to eke out a living.

Enter DUNMORE. *He saunters in sullenly, picks up a newspaper, and sits down at a table. He and* MARLOWE *bow distantly.* WAITER *enters and serves* DUNMORE.

Fan. Well met. The very man I wished to see. [*Takes pistol from his pocket and approaches* DUNMORE.] Good day, Captain.

Dun. Good day. [*Looking up.*] Hello, Dick! You here? Have a drink?

Fan. No, thanks. I only want to return this pistol that I—borrowed out of your hands last night during the rumpus at Mason's. I must apologize for not having stopped to ask your consent.

Dun., (*taking pistol*). It's all right, Dick, but I wish to God you had let me alone.

Fan. It was a very fortunate thing for you that I did not. [*Aside, as he walks back to table:* Or you would be playing the chief part in a hanging exhibition some weeks hence.]

Mar. Are you not putting a pistol into dangerous hands? That man is greatly struck with Miss Denham, and if he and the Colonel should meet here the consequences might be serious.

Fan. There is no danger. The man is the Colonel's nephew and is living on him. Besides, the pistol is not loaded. Look at him. He is interesting. He has been a pirate.

Mar. A pirate!

Fan. Yes; or slave-trader, which is the same thing. He wants me to join him in an expedition to the coast of Africa [*laughs*], to be his doctor.

Re-enter COL. VAUGHN *and* MISS DENHAM.

Fan. Here come the people we are waiting for. Now, while you engage the lady in conversation I will let the Colonel know who you are.

[COL. V. *and* MISS D. *come forward, meeting* FANSHAWE *and* MARLOWE, *who rise.' Salutations.* FANSHAWE *and* COL. V. *converse apart.* MISS D. *and* MARLOWE *walk aside.*

Miss D. George, you have come to see me?

Mar. I have. It is to let you know that what we feared has happened. The company have gone.

Miss D. I knew of it. The newspapers give full accounts of it. Oh, the humiliation! the disgrace! the shame! And now what is to be done?

Mar. There is but one thing to do that I can see. It is to make such terms as we can with our creditors, and then—— [*Aside:* Now, Heaven forgive me for the blow I must inflict.]

Miss D. Then what, George?

Mar. Separate, as the others have done. Bid each other farewell.

Miss D. Oh, no, George! do not say that. Let us remain together. We can give readings.

Mar. It cannot be, Aliena. There is not a dollar between us.

Miss D. But I have my wardrobe and some jewelry left. They will bring some money.

Mar. I will not touch a penny of it. It will enable you to reach your friends. Leave me to extricate myself. I will find some means of doing it.

Miss D. My friends! Alas, there is no one in this world who stands in that relation to me save you, and if you desert me I am desolate indeed.

Mar. Desertion is a harsh word, Aliena. It is not desertion, but hard, unyielding necessity that thrusts us apart. There is no help for it. It is fate. We must submit.

Miss D. Well, then, let us do so; but not to remain apart, George. Let us keep that hope between us.

Mar. Would it not be best, Aliena, that that hope should die? Come, let us look at the future we would have before us should we marry. What would it be but a hard and bitter struggle with poverty, from which there would be no hope of escape? Have you the courage to face a future so hopeless?

Miss D. I have. The future would be a dark one, but not so dark as the one from which love vanishes.

Mar. Aliena, I will not accept the sacrifice you would make for me. It would be criminal in me to do so. Separated from me, you have a future brilliant with promise. With me, nothing but a poverty that would make life a curse. So let us separate while we can—before it is too late.

Miss D. Well, perhaps it is best that we should part, George—if you think so. Where shall you go from here?

Mar. Perhaps I shall stay. I have met a friend here who proposes something that offers the hope of a better future, and—I think—it would be wise to—stay.

Miss D. Should you return to New York, would you go back to our old boarding-house?

Mar. I should, undoubtedly.

Miss D. Then we may meet again there. And if we should, and there should then be a brighter future for us, we might not—need—to part again.   [MARLOWE *does not answer.*

Miss D. [*Aside:* Ah, he doubts me—distrusts me! And so farewell to the dearest hope of my life. But better so, for the part that I have now to play—that I must play—there is no help for it. A loveless marriage.]

Fan., (*approaching Marlowe*). Good news, my friend. The Colonel is wonderfully surprised to learn who you are, and overjoyed to engage you. Tomorrow you are to begin your lessons. Now, come home to dinner with me. I want to have my father know you.

    [*Exeunt* FANSHAWE *and* MARLOWE, COL. V. *and* MARLOWE
      saluting.

Col. V., (*to* Miss D.). Well, upon my life, here is a most amazing revelation. Rugge, your leading man, turns out to be Marlowe, the artist, who so mysteriously disappeared some three years ago. Why, for what strange reason did he give up his art to take up with the life of a wandering player?

Miss D. For no strange reason at all. He failed to win success as an artist, and being poor was obliged to find some other means of earning a living, which he did, or tried to do, by taking to the stage. And perhaps his failure was somewhat due to the fact that he is an artist of an exceptional kind. He don't run all over the country to hunt up a rock, a landscape, or a tree, but paints the life that lays under his eyes.

Col. V. And paints it so well that he is not unworthy to wear the mantle of the master in whose path he follows. Well, his star shall shine again.

Miss D. [*Aside:* It shall, if your fortune can roll back the clouds that obscure it.]

Col. V. But let us put that subject aside for the moment for one in which I am more deeply interested. It is your intended departure. Do you still adhere to that determination?

Miss D. I do. I must. I have no alternative, and must depart at once. And now, sir, before we part, let me thank you for the rare kindness and courtesy you have shown me during my stay here. I shall never, never forget it.

Col. V. I am amply repaid in having been of any service to you. But what will you do, my dear lady? You are alone, and I think without money?

Miss D. Yes; I am alone, and without money.

Col. V. Miss Denham, I cannot permit you to depart in this distressed condition. You must allow me to assist you.

[DUNMORE *listens over the newspaper.*

Miss D. Dear sir, how can you do so? You could only offer me money. How can I accept that without humiliation from one who is almost a stranger?

Col. V. What! will you, rather than accept a favor that involves a little sacrifice of pride, go forth unfriended and alone to the desperate future that must await you?

Miss D. I will.

Col. V. You are a brave woman. [*Aside:* And not the woman I have taken you for. A woman of this stamp is certainly no adventuress. It only increases my admiration for her.] Let me see if I cannot find some way of assisting you, Miss Denham, without offending that sensitive pride, which, let me say, 1 respect and honor. If you would let me know what you intend on leaving here——

Miss D. It is to seek employment somewhere.

Col. V. And what then?

Miss D. Sink back into the obscurity and poverty from which I arose—or sought to arise—and become the music teacher again.

Col. V. A most disheartening prospect, truly. But you have shown me a way in which I can serve you. Such employment as you intend to seek can be found here in this city. Will you let me procure it for you?

Miss D. Gladly. And will give you the thanks of one lifted from the very depths of despair.

Col. V. And now I have one more request to urge—that you will become a guest in my house until the employment I shall seek for you is found. Do you consent?

Miss D. It is an honor, sir, that I cannot decline.

Col. V. Many a bright star of the stage have I entertained there—and there you shall shine the brightest of all. I have no wife, but I have a daughter who will most kindly welcome you.

[*Exeunt* Col. V. and Miss D. *As they go out, enter* John Carson, *from the veranda of the hotel. He salutes, and steps aside to permit* Miss D. *and* Col. V. *to pass, then turns and looks after* Miss D. *as if greatly surprised at seeing her. At the veranda exit* Miss D., *before going out, turns and glances back at* Carson.]

Carson, (*looking after* Miss D.) What! Can it be possible? That woman here? Yes, it is she, and no one else—Julia Montague, as I live! What, in the name of all that is wonderful, brings that woman to this town?

Dun. Don't you know, John?

Car., (*turning*). Hello, Jack; you here? No, I don't know. [*Coming down front.*]

Dun. Then you have not been to the theatre lately, I reckon.

Car. I have not been to the theatre in a month.

Dun. Then that accounts for your surprise at seeing the lady, doubtless. She is an actress here, or was—the leading lady of

3

a company that have been playing here for the past week—but have skipped out.

Car. An actress?

Dun. Yes. Miss Aliena Denham, she calls herself in the bills.

Car. An actress! Well, that is a new part for her—and a new name, too.

Dun. From your remarks, John, I would infer that you have had some previous acquaintance with the lady. [CARSON *takes seat at table with* DUN.]

Car. You would infer correctly. I have had some previous acquaintance with the lady. [*Waiter enters and serves liquor.*]

Dun. Well, who is she, and what is she, and under what interesting circumstances did you make her acquaintance? I am interested.

Car. Who she is is more than I can tell you. What she is is not so difficult to know. She is an adventuress, and one of the most brilliant and dangerous that it has ever been my good, or bad, fortune to fall in with.

Dun. Oh, come, John, this woman is no adventuress. She is too good an actress for that.

Car. An adventuress she is, or rather was when I knew her. That was in Albany during a session of the legislature, two years ago. She was not then an actress—at least not upon the stage— though she played a part in the social scene of the capital city, in which she was the heroine of as dark a tragedy as any she will ever enact upon the boards, I am thinking.

Dun. A tragedy! The interest deepens. What was the tragedy?

Car. Well, if I were to give it a name, I should call it after the part she played in it, that of a Siren of the Lobby. The tragedy was one that grew out of a lobby scheme, in which this woman had a part. The object of this plot was to secure the passage of a bill that a powerful railroad corporation was interested in. A certain member of the lower house stopped its passage, and as money could not remove his opposition this Miss Montague, or Miss Denham, was introduced upon the scene and employed to use her charms upon him. The scheme was a complete success. But it so happened that in removing his opposition she had enmeshed him in such a toil of passion that he

fell in love with and wanted to marry her; but this not being
in her part, she refused him. The poor, infatuated man, dis-
covering that he had been made the victim of a plot and also
the victim of a hopeless passion for an adventuress, took the
matter so much to heart that he killed himself.

Dun. Poor devil! Rather an odd kind of lawmaker, it seems
to me. [*Aside:* And it is my notion that my noble friend here
must have had a part in the business if he was anywhere upon
the scene.] You were a member of that session, were you not,
John?

Car. I was; but its reminiscences are not pleasant, so let us
change the subject. I have come here to meet your uncle, the
Colonel, and when he reappears just make it convenient to leave
me alone with him, will you?

Dun. The Colonel will not reappear today, and I'm thinking
you will not see him for the next month.

Car. No? Why not?

Dun. Because he will be engaged with your Siren of the
Lobby, this Miss Montague, or Miss Denham, or whatever her
name is. Her company have skipped off, and the Colonel has
taken her to his house as his guest!

Car. What! His guest? Then the Colonel is a lost man.

Dun. A lost man? What do you mean by a lost man?

Car. I mean that she will marry him if she should wish to.
She will inspire him with a passion so deep that if the cup of
bliss is only to be reached through the matrimonial noose he
will take it.

Dun. And trust to a divorce court lawyer to pull him out of
it when he gets down to the dregs, eh? That seems to be the
way in the North. But don't you think you could prevent the
marriage by telling the Colonel that story about her that you
have just told me?

Car. I might, if I were mean enough to let him know it.

Dun. What would there be mean about it?

Car. It would be a betrayal of the woman. I was not altogether blameless in that lobby business. I am bound in honor
to keep her secret, and will do so unless forced to reveal it.

Dun. With the object of frightening her off?

Car. No; it will be with the object of making her useful in
averting the financial ruin that threatens me.

Dun. What do you say? Financial ruin! Are you threatened with that?

Car. I am; and unless I can find the means of averting it within the next thirty days I shall have to fly the country or go to the State prison.

Dun. Good God, John, are you serious?

Car. I was never more so, Jack. I am on the verge of bankruptcy, and what is worse, disgrace.

Dun. What, you! Why, what in the devil's name——

Car. Oh, it is the old story—Wall street—stock speculation. I went down in the last panic with thousands of others. To save myself I have embezzled the bank's resources to such an extent that unless I can make good the deficit within the next month the doors will have to be closed.

Dun. Well, John, you are a thoroughbred; you never do anything by halves. Well, what are you going to do if the crash comes? Take the usual course and run for it?

Car. No; I shall take the unusual course—stay and face the consequences.

Dun. What, go to jail?

Car. Possibly; but not until after I have made an effort to save myself. I have a plan by which I may be able to do so.

Dun. Namely?

Car. I am going to get married.

Dun. Marry, eh? Instead of the prison chains, put on the matrimonial fetters, eh? It strikes me they will rest rather heavily on a man who has been a free ranger like you. It is some woman with much money and no charms besides, I suppose?

Car. It is one of the richest heiresses and the most lovely woman in the State.

Dun. So! Then I can guess who it is. It is my cousin Rose.

Car. It is. The marriage has been pending for some time — a sort of family understanding that we were to marry some day. Rose has only been waiting for me to make up my mind. And now, Jack, I want you to spread the news of the engagement. That will postpone failure, and the marriage will save me.

Dun. I will spread the news, you may depend. But there is something in this connection which, as your friend, I think I ought to tell you. Come, pay attention. You seem to be mightily distrait. This is a damned uncertain world, you know.

Car. It is. Well?

Dun. Rose is not the legitimate heir of her father.

Car. What do you mean?

Dun. Well, thereby hangs a tale. Do you remember my telling you about a month ago of the Colonel's betrayal and ruin of a young woman—the daughter of a high family of Alabama—when he was a resident of that State?

Car. Yes; I remember something of it.

Dun. Well, who do you suppose that young woman was? She was my aunt—my father's sister; and, furthermore, she was the mother of Rose.

Car. Indeed?

Dun. Soon after Rose's birth she died—died in a negro cabin on the Colonel's estate, to which she had fled on leaving her home. Before she died the Colonel had married her. But it was too late. Rose was born before the marriage ceremony took place. So, you see, if the Colonel should die without leaving a will the estate would go to the next legal heir—who sits before you. The affair led to a vendetta between the families, in which several men were killed on each side, and to save his own life and the life of his daughter the Colonel left Alabama and settled in this region, where he had some relatives among the Fanshawes.

Car. So, Jack, I thank you for the information.

Dun. And now, I suppose that ivory and ebony scheme of mine will have to be given up?

Car. Yes; if you mean that slave-trading adventure that you want me to advance the capital for. That will have to be given up for the present, Jack. I cannot raise another dollar.

Dun. It is too bad. There is a mint of money in the trade.

Car. What made you give it up, if it was so profitable?

Dun. Some bad luck at cards one night in Savannah. I lost my schooner and had to discharge my crew. It was with the hope of raising some capital from my uncle, the Colonel, that I paid him a visit last summer.

Car. Can't you get the money from him?

Dun. I may be able to do so next month, when he opens his house to his summer guests. He has partly promised to let me have it.

Car. But the trade is piracy under our laws, Jack, and a man swings for it if caught.

Dun. The laws be hanged. A dozen slavers leave the port of New York every year, and have for the last hundred years. I can dodge a cruiser as easily as tack ship, and have done it often. So much for the danger.

Re-enter MISS DENHAM. *She goes to a table on which she had left a veil and some flowers and takes them up.*

Dun. Ah, John, here comes your Siren of the Lobby back again. She has recognized you, doubtless, and perhaps wants an interview with you.

Car. It may be. It is what I want with her above all things. [*Approaches and salutes* MISS D.] Ah, Miss Montague, I am extremely glad to meet you. Until today I was not aware of your presence in town.

[MISS D. *does not answer, but looks steadily at* CARSON.

Car. I assure you, Miss Montague, that this opportunity of renewing an acquaintance connected with such pleasant associations is most welcome.

Miss D. Mr. Carson, perhaps I can understand why you should regard the associations you speak of as pleasing; but to me, sir, they are the most painful recollections of my life, and I would gladly avoid all occasions that bring them to mind.

Car. But, Miss Montague, you mistake me.

Miss D. Evidently, sir, you mistake me.

Car. I think not, Miss—Montague; and let me say that under present circumstances it is not advisable for you to take this tone with me. It might be embarrassing to you hereafter.

Miss D. It is a tone that I shall take with you, sir, under any circumstances, now or hereafter.

Car. So! Is this defiance?

Miss D. As you may choose to regard it.

They stand regarding each other as the curtain descends, MISS D. *defiantly,* CARSON *as if surprised.*

ACT II.—A MONTH LATER.

SCENE—*Country Residence of* COL. VAUGHN. *On left, veranda of house fronting garden. Vista of trees and shrubbery. Under a tree an easel, before which stands* MARLOWE, *palette and brush in hand, regarding a picture.* JUDGE CROTCHET *seated apart reading.*

Enter FANSHAWE *from the house. Approaches* MARLOWE *and lays his hand upon his shoulder.*

Mar., (*turning*). What, Fanshawe! You at last? Why, you are a strange fellow, to leave me here for a month without letting me know what had become of you. I was beginning to think that something very serious had happened to you.

Fan. Nothing more serious than hard work. I have been rushing to completion a novel I had under way. But that is finished, thank the Lord, and now here I am, ready to collaborate with you in the progress of that romance in actual life that we projected in the garden of that tavern a month ago. How is it getting on?

Mar. Well, I can't say that the romance, as you choose to call it, is progressing very brilliantly.

Fan. Indeed! And why not?

Mar. For the reason that I find the part you gave me more difficult to enact than I anticipated. I know I promised to undertake it, but when I did so I was so desperate with misfortune that I would have undertaken almost anything short of actual crime to escape from the life I was leading and the future before me. Now——

Fan. Oh, I understand. Now that the road to success leads some other way, and the lady is not to your liking——

Mar. Oh, do not mistake me, my dear friend. The difficulty of the part does not lie there. Nothing in the world would be so dear to me as the hope of winning Miss Vaughn—one as gifted in mind and heart as she is lovely in person—and one whom I must confess I find it almost impossible not to love.

Fan. Then why do you hesitate?

Mar. My friend, you do not seem to consider my position

here. I am in her father's employ—a guest in his house. He has loaded me with favor, caused me to be honored beyond my desert. Then how can I with honor undertake to win his daughter's love when it might not suit him and when he favors another man?

Fan. My dear boy, you put too low an estimate upon yourself; you do, indeed. Why, you are a match for the proudest family in the land. Then why not suppress a little of this all too sensitive pride and save the woman you love—for I am certain that you love her—from a man who would make her life miserable should he marry her?

Mar. Can I do so? It may be she loves this man Carson; and certainly her father favors him.

Fan. I do not believe she loves him. And yet there lies my fear, too. The noblest women seem to have such an alacrity in throwing themselves away upon scamps. But I mean to find out this day if she loves him, and if she does not, and is free for you to win, will you go on with the part?

Mar. I will; and if she gives the least encouragement I will do my best to win her.

Fan. Then cheer up, faint heart. I am certain that you will win her, and I predict that within the year you will be married, and here in this noble mansion take up your abode and go on to the success and fame that I am certain await you; and then your country will hear of a great artist some time before he is dead.

Mar. You are such a courageous spirit! Your very contact inspires a man with hope. But let me tell you that you are reckoning without your host, so far as the noble mansion is concerned. That is already bespoken for a pair of lovers.

Fan. Indeed! And what pair?

Mar. For Colonel Vaughn and his intended wife, Miss Denham.

Fan. What! The Colonel and Miss Denham?

Mar. It is even so. They are engaged, and the Colonel has already announced his coming marriage to some of his guests, and will make a more formal announcement today. Does the marriage surprise you?

Fan. No; on second thought, I cannot say that it does, considering the circumstances that have brought such a man and such a woman together.

Mar. She is not an unworthy woman, my friend.

Fan. I would not imply that she is. Know you aught of her history?

Mar. Nothing beyond the two years' acquaintance that I have had with her. I first met her in a New York boarding-house. She was then a music teacher, and studying for the stage. She fell into the hands of the same theatrical adventurer who sought me out. There was a time when I was somewhat doubtful concerning her, but the more I understand her the more I am convinced that she is a woman of really noble char-acter. Of her past life she says little.

Fan. How does Rose regard the coming marriage of her father?

Mar. She does not seem displeased with it. She and Miss Denham appear to be excellent friends.

Fan. Then she certainly regards Miss Denham as worthy to be her father's wife. And that is enough. And here comes the angel.

Enter ROSE VAUGHN *and* MISS BELLE DUNMORE. *They are fol-lowed by some guests, who gather about the easel.* MISS VAUGHN *and* MISS DUNMORE *come forward, meeting* FANSHAWE *and* MARLOWE.

Rose V. Why, here is my dear brother Richard at last—my long-lost brother. And where have you been, truant, for so long? Though I do not suppose I need ask. You have been at your old labor, doubtless, adding the sum of more to that which hath too much—which means that you have been writ-ing another novel.

Fan. You have guessed it.

Rose. Well, tell us all about it, and be forgiven. What is it like? We are sadly in want of amusement.

Fan. Well, it is like other novels that are like it.

Rose. Then it is like the rest of your novels, I suppose—one giving a false color to life and making a dismal world appear bright and joyous—all ending happily, with virtue rewarded and the villain out in the cold. Is your new novel after this fashion?

Fan. Somewhat.

Rose. Then don't tell us anything about it. I am tired of

4

such novels. Why don't you portray men and women as they are and life as it is—give us heroes and heroines who have their faults, like other folks, and villains with some redeeming qualities. It is so in actual life, though precious few of you novel-writers seem to have found it out. And why don't you take the subjects for your novels, as Mr. Marlowe does for his pictures, from the life you live in ?

Fan. Well, for one reason, because I don't find the life I live in very rich in romantic material.

Rose. Then you ought never to write another novel. What! no romance, no story element, in the life of a country where Fortune's lists are open to all comers, where all the prizes of life are within the reach of the man who has the brains and the courage to enter for them; where a tinker who goes West may return a Senator—like Mr. Brownsmith over there—and where a shoemaker's apprentice may become President! No romance, no dramatic material in such a life ! Why, it is a life that Shakespeare would have revelled in, so full as it is of the ups and downs of fortune, of heroic action, of the display of character and human nature in the struggles of men making their way from low to high station, from obscurity to renown, through a thousand fields of activity and adventure. Here, [*taking a newspaper from a table,*] take this dramatic kaleidoscope, the American newspaper, and write me a play from it within the next month.

Fan. I will, and will put your speech into it. But before I begin it I want to know how a little romance in real life that I am interested in is likely to end. [*Aside :* And now to discover what truth there is in her reported engagement to Carson.]

Rose. Oh, then, it seems you have discovered some romance in real life?

Fan. Yes; and I can't sleep nights for anxiety as to how it is going to turn out. I want you to tell me. You see there is a young artist who is very poor, who is in love with a young lady who is very rich. On account of his poverty he keeps his love a secret.

Rose. Poor young man! But what kind of an artist is he? All are not artists who are called such, you know.

Fan. He is a man of genius!

Rose. But has he got any common sense? Genius without that quality is like a ship without ballast. It makes a wavering, inconstant man and a bad husband.

Fan. He is not lacking in common sense.

Rose. Well, then, if he is a good man and she likes him, she would be a great fool not to have him.

Fan. But there is a rival to whom it is said she is engaged.

Rose. A villain, of course!

Fan. No, not exactly a villain. To the world he is a gentleman, but in private life he is very much of a scamp.

Rose. Has the girl got any brains?

Fan. She is as gifted in mind as she is beautiful in person.

Rose. Then it is not difficult to see how your romance is likely to end. She will discover the love of the artist and find some delicate, womanly way of letting him know she likes him, and she will discover the scampishness of the scamp and send him packing. [*Aside:* And it is my opinion that she has done it already.] And so all will end happily.

Fan. Ah, my dear cousin, how glad I am to hear this! You see, she is an angel, and you know how prone angels are to throw themselves away upon scamps—through missionary motives, I suppose.

Rose. If she has got brains she isn't that kind of an angel. So don't worry. And now, speaking of angels—I mean artists—how is it that Mr. Marlowe——

Enter from the house Col. Vaughn *and* Miss Denham. *They are followed by* Guests, *who gather about the easel. Following them, enter* Carson *and* Dunmore, *who come forward.* Col. V., Miss D., Fanshawe, Judge Crotchet, Rose, *and* Belle Dunmore *in a group apart on* L. Guests *express admiration for the picture and offer congratulations to* Marlowe. Carson *seems thoughtful and depressed.*

Fan., (*to Rose*). Now, what were you about to say concerning Mr. Marlowe?

Rose. I was going to ask you to explain why so great an artist as he is should fail to win success in his profession—for a great artist he certainly is. Look at the portrait he has painted of me. Why, he has made me immortal.

Fan. Yes, I could explain the cause of his failure, but the Judge can do it better. Ask him. Since his defeat in the last election he loses no opportunity to uncork the vials of his wrath

upon his country and its institutions. That subject will afford
him an opportunity and us some sport.

[ROSE *and* MISS DUNMORE *turn to the* JUDGE.   FANSHAWE *calls
    the attention of* COL. V. *and the* GUESTS *to them, and unob-
    served by the* JUDGE *they gather behind him to listen.*

Rose.   Come, Judge [*taking his arm*], you heard my question
and cousin Dick's answer.

Judge.   Yes, I heard the jackanapes. Well, my dear, it is my
opinion that Mr. Marlowe's failure to win success as an artist
was due to the fact that he was too poor to emigrate to a foreign
country.

Rose.   Emigrate to a foreign country? Must our American
artists do that in order to win success?

Judge.   It seems that they must, my dear. The fact that so
many of them go there, and that we never hear of them until
they have won a reputation in Europe, seems pretty good proof
of it.

Rose.   Why, Judge, I can scarcely believe it. Is it possible—
is it absolutely necessary that an artist must go abroad for that
purpose?

Judge.   Well, my dear, I can't say that it is absolutely necessary. He might stay at home and buy a reputation from the
newspapers in his own country.

Rose.   Buy a reputation from the newspapers? Can that be
done?

Judge.   Can that be done? Why, certainly, my dear—by
means of a press agent. Let him do as some of the foreign lit-
erary and theatrical people do who come to this country for our
dollars—put himself in the hands of a press agent. One of that
gentry could take the painter of a mere auction-room pot-boiler
and make him out to be the equal of a Hogarth or a Rembrandt,
and, what is more, he could make our millionaire art patrons, who
pay fortunes for the rubbish of European studios with some
great name attached, pay some attention to him. It is only the
trumpets and drums of the advertiser, my dear, that bring success to art in our democratic vanity fair.

Rose.   But go a little more into causes, Judge. Why is it that
the artist has a better chance for recognition and success in Europe than in America?   [*Nodding to* FANSHAWE.

Judge.   In my opinion, it is due to the difference in the social conditions of Europe and America, which gives to the artist over there what he lacks here, a constituency in a permanent and cultured leisure class.

Rose. Why, Judge, I could almost think that you are a believer in an aristocracy.

Judge. Well, whatever I may think of an aristocracy, my dear, I am pretty certain that as the foster nurse of art and of everything else that confers greatness and glory upon a nation, it is much better than the unmitigated democracy that we have adopted.

Fan. Hear the statesman!

Judge, (turning). Oh, you heard me, did you, and I have got an audience, have I? Well, ladies and gentlemen, I will not take back a word. As regards aristocracy, I am not ashamed to share William Shakespeare's opinion on that subject, and if he was not a believer in aristocracy, and the most intense that ever lived, then I am an idiot.

Fan., (jestingly). Well, if here isn't an open and avowed emissary of the Man on Horseback! Colonel, have a rope prepared, and we will take him to a tree.

Col. V. No, let him go on, Dick. We don't think of taking him seriously since the last election. It is the old story, ladies and gentlemen. The Judge is a defeated candidate. [*Laughter.*]

Judge. Laugh, on, Colonel, while you can. If that is the way with defeated candidates, your turn may come. I understand that you are a candidate for Congress.

Col. V. Then let me correct you, Judge. I am not a candidate for Congress. It was my intention to be a candidate, but I have altered my mind, and shall not accept the nomination.

Judge. Indeed, Colonel! This will be a great surprise to your party friends. Do you object to giving your reasons for declining?

Col. V. Not at all. It is for the very best reason in the world. I am going to be married.

Judge. Well, that certainly is a good reason. An election canvass cannot be regarded as the sweetener of a candidate's honeymoon.

Col. V. It shall not embitter mine. And now let me formally present to you and to all of my guests the lady who is to be my wife—Miss Aliena Denham. Our acquaintance has not been long, it is true, but it has been long enough to let me know her as one of the noblest of women, and in making her my wife I shall make myself one of the happiest of men.

Judge. Well, Colonel, let me congratulate you on the possession of so fair a bride.

[GUESTS *gather around* COL. V. *and* MISS D. *and offer congratulations.*

Dunmore (to Carson, rousing him). Ah, John! Do you hear this?

Carson. Yes; I hear it. It does not surprise me. It was what I expected.

Dun. Well, let him marry her. I give my consent. It will give a piquancy to dull family life to have a woman around that a man would be willing to go to the devil for.

Car. Which is the very thing that you would do if the opportunity should offer.

Dun. I am bound to admit that I would go a long way in that direction for such a woman as she is.

Car. Better not let your thoughts run that way, Jack. It will not do for you.

Dun. I know it, John; and I am going to get out of the way. Besides, it is of no use of my staying around here any longer, anyhow.

Car. Can you not raise the capital from the Colonel for your slave-trading adventure?

Dun. I cannot. I was on the point of getting it, but Rose heard what it was wanted for, and she went to her father with some remarks about the hellish traffic, and he tore up the check that was almost within my grasp. [*Aside:* Curse her, if I don't get even with her for this I hope to rot alive.] And that is not the only thing I have against her. I could have married my cousin Belle had it not been for her. But look here, John; you might raise the capital from Miss Denham after she is married to the Colonel. With that knowledge of her past that you possess she would be willing to do for you so small a favor as that. Do you see those diamonds that she wears? They are a gift from the Colonel and are worth fifty thousand dollars—so the women say.

Car. There is no certainty that she is going to marry the Colonel.

Dun. Then you think of telling him that story about her that you told me?

Car. I can't say now what I shall do. It will depend upon the result of a private interview that I intend to have with her. If she consents to do what I shall ask of her, I shall remain silent. If not, I go to the Colonel with her story.

Dun. She looks to me like a woman who don't scare easily, John.

Car. Then I shall have another card to play that will bring her to terms—something that I have discovered since.

Dun. What does it happen to be?

Car. It happens to be the fact that she is in love with the artist Marlowe.

Dun. The deuce you say! How did you discover that?

Car. She betrayed herself. I suspected that she might be in love with Marlowe, and for the past two days I have watched her and have noticed that whenever he has been in her presence her eyes have constantly followed him about. It seems to be an unconscious action with her. He don't stir but her eyes follow and rest upon him with a half sad, half reproachful gaze. If that don't indicate love I know nothing of women. She loves him and loves him intensely.

Dun. Is Marlowe in love with her?

Car. No; he is in love with some one else—as I have discovered by watching him.

Dun. With whom else?

Car. With Rose.

Dun. You have a rival, then?

Car. Yes, and a successful one. Rose has broken off the engagement. Some recent scandal concerning me had reached her ears, and when I could not deny that it was true she plainly told me that my proposal of marriage was an insult, and advised me to go and marry my last mistress.

Dun. By the gods! did she say that? [*Laughter.*] Well, what are you going to do? Give her up?

Car. Give her up? No, not while my name is John Carson! I cannot give her up. I must marry her. It is the only means by which I can save myself from ruin and disgrace.

Dun. But what are you going to do?

Car. What I am going to do, Jack, is what you must not

know. But first of all, I must have an interview with Miss Denham. She has avoided me so far, but we must now come to an understanding. [*Approaches Miss D.* DUNMORE *edges around and listens.*] Miss Denham, permit me to offer my congratulations on your coming marriage. I do so most sincerely, and wish you happiness with all my heart.

Miss D., (*coldly*). I thank you, sir.

Car. Miss Denham, there is a matter of some importance about which I wish to speak with you—alone. Can you grant me an interview for that purpose?

Miss D. I cannot, sir. Whatever you wish to say to me, Mr. Carson, must be said here, or in the presence of others.

Car. But it concerns a matter upon which I cannot speak in the presence of others.

Miss D. Then, sir, I cannot hear it.

Car. Miss Denham, it cannot be possible that you misunderstand me. You must know upon what subject I wish to speak. Am I to understand that you defy me?

Miss D. You can so understand me, sir, if your words imply any threat.

Car. They imply that I shall have a duty to do by a friend unless you grant me the interview I ask for. What that may mean you cannot fail to understand.

Miss D. Do that duty, sir, and then perhaps I shall have a duty to do. What that may mean perhaps you may be able to understand. [*Turns away.*]

Car. By the gods, she is bold! What can make her so defiant? Does she imagine that I do not know the ending of that terrible drama in which she played the heroine? If she does she must be undeceived, and it shall be done here and now.

Dun. [*Aside:* As I expected, she is a fighter; and now the sport begins.]

Miss D. [*Aside:* Can it be possible that this man can be so base as to betray me? I cannot believe it, for to do so would be to paint himself black with villainy and shame. It cannot be that he knows of the fate of poor Doughton, so I have nothing to fear from any revelations that he may make.]

Car., (*approaching Judge*). Judge, I want you to do me a favor. I am going to make a speech here, and perhaps in that connection I shall have a story to tell. What I want is to have you lead the conversation up to it, so that I can bring it in. Do you understand me?

Judge. Perfectly.

Car. Well; now go to the Colonel and urge him to reconsider his decision not to accept the nomination for Congress. That is going to cause a great deal of confusion. In that connection, speak of your experience in the State legislature of two years ago. Dwell strongly upon that, for that will be the cue for the speech I intend to make.

Judge. All right, John, I will follow your instructions. [*Aside:* And perhaps I'll better them.] [*They walk back to* Col. V.]

Judge (to Col. V.) Colonel, excuse me. I want a word upon a matter that will admit of no delay. Are you aware that your withdrawal from the canvass is going to be the cause of a great deal of trouble to your party friends?

Col. V. I cannot see why, Judge. The nomination is not yet made. So far as I am concerned, I would be willing to accept the nomination, but it is against the wishes of my intended wife, and it is also against the wishes of my daughter, so I will not alter my mind now.

Judge. Well, then, Colonel, if you will not, that ends it. And I cannot say that, political duty aside, you do not take the wisest course. It would not increase your wife's happiness or your daughter's to have you denounced as one of the greatest villains that ever lived. Oh, the rancors of a party contest! I know what they are, ladies and gentlemen. I have been a candidate. In that canvass I was a gambler, a cut-throat, and a horse-thief. And after a man wins his election—if he don't get cheated out of it—what is he brought in contact with? A trickery, a conspiracy, a bartering away of the rights of the people, and a strife for spoils that develops all that is mean and villainous in human nature.

Car. Come, Judge, you need not be so sweeping in your denunciation. You are laying it on too thick. Don't take your defeat so much to heart.

Judge. You mind your own business, John. I know what I am talking about.

Car. But your condemnation is too general. You have in your mind the legislative session of two years ago, of which you were a member—and so was I. It gained a bad reputation, but as a body it was composed of honest men.

5

Judge. So are they all composed of honest men in the main. But what chance have the honest men against the boodlers, the bosses, and the lobbyists that infest them? About the same chance they would have in a game against a stocked pack. You know as well as I do that no legislation can be had without a compromise with such rascals. It is that which casts such a stigma upon our State legislative bodies, which makes our American politics the scandal of the world, the terror of liberty. As to this particular session you were speaking of, I was a member of it, and if I didn't think I deserved the State prison for being found in some of the company I was obliged to forgather with, I am a Tombs lawyer.

Car. I must agree with you, Judge, as to that body. And it was not alone villainy of a vulgar character that distinguished it. It was made memorable by one of the darkest tragedies that I think I ever heard or even read of. [*Looking at Miss Denham.*]

Judge. A tragedy, John? What tragedy? I heard of none connected with that session.

Car. No, Judge; you did not hear of it. It was kept secret, so far as that could be done.

Judge. Relate it, John.

Car. No, Judge; I had much rather not. It is too sad a story, and throws such a lurid light upon some of our methods of legislation that I think I ought, for the sake of patriotism, to say nothing about it.

Judge. Oh, hang the patriotism. Give us the tragedy.

A Lady Guest. Do tell it, Mr. Carson.

Another Lady. Do let us hear it.

Third Lady. Do, Mr. Carson.

Col. V. John, you have aroused the curiosity of the ladies. You will have to tell the story.

Car. Very well, then, ladies, if you insist upon hearing the story, I must comply, of course, but I think you will wish that you had not heard it. Well, this tragedy that I speak of was one that grew out of the plottings of the lobby that gathered around that session that we were speaking of. The object of these plottings was to secure the passage of a bill that a powerful railroad corporation was interested in. The bill was apparently a very innocent one, and was on the point of becoming a law, when its progress was abruptly checked by a member, who

in a speech took it to pieces and showed that, cunningly stowed
away in its clauses, was a scheme to defraud the State. This
member was a man named Doughton. He was the hero and,
I may say, the victim of the tragedy. His speech apparently
killed the bill, but as great interests depended on its passage, the
railroad corporation determined to get it through at all costs.
Through their agents in the lobby they brought their influence
to bear in removing the opposition of Doughton. First, they
tried what money could do. That failed. Doughton proved
himself beyond its influence. Then party discipline was tried.
That failed also. Then patronage; then personal friendship;
then wine; but each proved fruitless. He was not to be reached
by influences such as these. Doughton was a scholar and a
gentleman— in that body to guard the rights of the people, as
he said, not to traffic in them. The lobby were in despair, and
were about to abandon their efforts to get the bill through, when
an accidental discovery revealed to them that the incorruptible
legislator did have a vulnerable side to his character after all.
As soon as this discovery was made the lobby changed their
tactics, and now began the real business of the tragedy. The
day on which this discovery of the weak side of Doughton's
character was made he received an invitation to be present that
evening at a reception to be given at the house of a prominent
Senator of that session, who was secretly interested in the passage of the bill that Doughton had opposed. He accepted and
·attended the reception. He found himself in a most brilliant
company, resplendent with fair women ; but conspicuous above
all for beauty, and for an easy, high-bred air that distinguished
her, was a lady from New York city, a Miss Julia Montague, a
relative of the Senator's family, or who was represented as such.
She was certainly the star of that assemblage, and would have
been conspicuous in any company in the world—not so much
for classical purity of feature, perhaps, but for the character in
her face, the expression of her eyes, and the irresistible charm
of her smile. She was another Récamier. To this lady Doughton was presented by his host, the Senator. He found her company so agreeable that he did not leave her side for the whole
evening. Miss Montague seemed equally pleased with him.
When he left he asked permission to repeat his visit. It was
granted ; and for many an evening after that and for many an

afternoon he was to be found by the side of Miss Montague.
But there is little use in lingering over the story. What happened was that which always happens when two intellectual
and sympathetic natures meet. Doughton was soon in the
siren's power and moulded to her will, and one day, not long
after he had met Miss Montague, he arose in his seat in the
committee-room and announced that he withdrew his opposition to the bill, and even went so far as to say a few words in
its favor. That settled its fate. That very day it became a law.
With this Miss Montague's work was done, and she took her pay
and quit the scene; for you must now understand, ladies and
gentlemen, that this woman was no relative of the Senator's
family at all, but a brilliant and fascinating adventuress, who
had been introduced upon the scene by the leaders of the lobby
with the object of beguiling Doughton of his opposition to the
bill. I wish I could say that my story ended here, for what
followed is too painful to relate. The siren had done her work
too well. In weaving her snares around Doughton she had enmeshed the unsuspecting man in a toil of passion and fascination that he could not throw off, and when she left he followed
her. He told her that for her sake he was willing to give up
everything and go with her to the ends of the earth. Poor
fellow! He felt that he was going to meet a passion as deep
and responsive as his own. He was not long in being undeceived. She told him that she did not love him, and that instead of being what she had seemed, she had only been employed to deceive him; that she was, in fact, a female lobbyist.
Doughton's blood almost froze in his veins as he listened to
her. When he left her it was as a broken man. The victim of
a legislative lobby, ensnared by an adventuress, tricked and
betrayed, laughed at and jeered at as he knew he would be, the
sensitive, proud gentleman had not the strength to return and
wear his disgrace in the face of the world. For two days he
wandered about the city, distraught with passion, shame, and
remorse, and when he could endure it no longer he went to an
obscure hotel, where the next morning, in a room in which he
had shut himself, he was found stretched upon his bed with a
bullet through his brain—dead by his own hand.

[*A momentary silence, which is broken by expressions of pity
among the women.*]

Miss D. [*Aside:* Ah, I am betrayed. This man knows everything—knows what I supposed was known only to myself—the death of poor Doughton. I am in his power and must submit.] *To Carson:* Mr. Carson, your story is indeed a sorrowful one, and interests me deeply, so much so that I would be glad to know what became of this—Miss—Montague. [*Touches his arm with her fan, and they unobserved draw aside.*]

Car. I can tell you this much—here—concerning her. After Doughton's death she disappeared and was heard of no more—as Julia Montague. Where she is now and what name she bears is to be a subsequent revelation, which will be made here, before this company, if you do not grant me the interview I ask for.

Miss D. I will grant it to you. Meet me here a half hour hence—alone. Dinner will soon be served. Do not go in. Among so many guests you will not be missed. I will plead illness and rejoin you.

[*They separate and retire back. A servant enters and announces that dinner is served.* Col. V. *leads the way with* Miss D., *followed by the* Guests. Carson *remains upon the scene.*

Car. And so the first card is down in the desperate game; and what is it for? Staking the substance, honor, against the shadow, reputation; and if I win, I lose the substance. Well, there is no help for it. It must be played to the bitter end.

Re-enter Miss Denham. *She stands back, regarding* Carson *for a moment, then comes forward.*

Miss D. Oh, you scoundrel! You heartless, conscienceless scoundrel! You mean scoundrel! If you have one spark of honor left—if you are not utterly lost to a sense of shame, how could you be so base, so vile, as to tell my story? You, the secret director of that lobby—you who contrived the plot to entrap poor Doughton's honor, and which ended in entrapping his soul, how dare you betray me, your confederate and victim? Yes, your victim! You know that by concealing from me the devilish nature of the work I was doing, by tempting my poverty, by opening to me a way of escape from the wretched life I was leading, you lured me into a participation in that villainy. And now, when I had fled from the shame and desolation it brought upon me—when I had found a refuge where by a life of sacrifice and good deeds I might make atonement and find peace, you come to drive me from it, and by an act so mean that the devils in hell would scorn you.

Car. Miss Denham, a desperate man may be driven to do what from his very soul he abhors. I am a desperate man, made so by the threatened loss of what is dearer to me than aught else in life—so dear that it has driven me to resort to any means that may save me. That I may do by your aid. Give me that aid and you can become the wife of Herbert Vaughn. Refuse it, and I will be guilty of the meanness of revealing to him and his guests the identity of Julia Montague with Aliqua Denham.

Miss D. It is your silence, then, that I must purchase?

Car. Yes.

Miss D. And by what means?

Car. That you are not to know until the time comes to do the work that I shall require of you. What it may be you may partly surmise when I say that a man has stepped between me and the woman I love.

Miss D. You have a rival, then, whom you wish to have removed?

Car. Yes. But be not alarmed; I mean neither steel nor poison.

Miss D. Is he among the guests?

Car. He is the artist, Marlowe.

Miss D. What, sir! George Marlowe? I do not believe it. It is not true.

Car. [*Aside:* Ah, that shot found its mark. She loves him, and now she will do my work.] You do not believe it? Have you been so blind as not to see that he and Rose Vaughn are in love?

Miss D. I have not been blind to the fact, sir, that George Marlowe is a gentleman, and would not secretly seek to win the love of the daughter of the man in whose house he is employed.

Car. Place no reliance upon that. What is honor in a conflict with love? Love would triumph; there would be a secret marriage, and so an end of my hopes.

Miss D. [*Aside:* It may be that he loves her. Well, let it be so. I must give him up.]

Car. And that marriage must be prevented, or ruin and disgrace await me. It can be done with your aid. Give me that aid, and tonight, in her father's house, before him and his guests, shall be enacted a scene that shall separate Rose and Marlowe forever and leave her free for me to win.

Miss D. And what part am I to enact in this scene?

Car. It will be one which, I regret to say, will require all your nerve and perhaps involve a little criminality.

Miss D. Then, sir, we can bring this interview to a close. Go to Herbert Vaughn; tell him and his guests that Aliena Denham and Julia Montague are the same. Drive me from here in disgrace. Do your worst; and be certain that I shall not fail to do mine.

Car. [*Aside*: She means it, and if she remains firm the game is up. I will not betray her. And now to play my last card— her love for Marlowe.] Do not be so mad, Miss Denham, as to refuse to do the work I ask of you. You do not realize the ruin it would bring upon you; and if you do as I wish, there is a happiness in store for you of which you do not dream. I mean that Herbert Vaughn's life is destined to be short. He has a malady which is certain to end his life within two years, and now any prolonged mental or emotional strain would snap his thread of life suddenly. He does not know this, but I know it from his physician. And suppose he should be thus cut off after he is married to you, what a future would then be yours! Mistress of his wealth, the world at your feet, and George Marlowe free for you to win. Ah, you love that man. I know your secret. Do my work—aid me to recover the woman he has taken from me, and he is yours.

Miss D. Oh, you scoundrel! you devil! How dare you make such a proposition to me? Out of my sight! I will no longer listen to you!

Car. [*Aside:* But you do listen, and the poison works. An hour hence and you will be willing to do my work.] Well, I will now leave you to think over what I have said. I will await your answer in the library. [*Exit, L., among the trees.*

Miss D. Oh, the accursed villain! I could kill him! I could kill him! [*Exit, R.*

Enter FANSHAWE *and* MARLOWE, *from the house.*

Fan. Now for one of the greatest of sublunary pleasures—an after-dinner chat and smoke under the greenwood tree.

[*They take seats and light cigars.*

Enter JUDGE C., *singing a merry air.*

Judge. Ah, my lads, here you are, eh? Escaped from the after-dinner oratory and the eternal slavery question, eh? Sensible boys!   [*Sits down.*

Fun. Have a cigar, Judge?

Judge. No, sir, I will not have a cigar. I have just eaten a civilized dinner, and the bliss of digestion is not to be poisoned by tobacco. Just now I am at peace with all the world. Ten whiffs of tobacco smoke and I could bite off a tenpenny nail. I have come here for coffee, which will soon be served.

Fun. And while we are waiting, suppose you give us some information. Being the Colonel's lawyer, you can doubtless give it. Who is Miss Denham?

Judge. That, sir, is information that I can supply only to a limited extent. She is a native of this State, the daughter of a country clergyman. On the death of her father she went into the world to earn her living by teaching in families. It was a hard life, from which she sought to escape by taking to the stage, in which venture she lost her friends and her money too. She has letters, which she has submitted to Rose, from certain high families, who recommend her highly as to character and ability. She is all right in every way. She is a superior woman. Beauty is the smallest of her charms. One half hour of her company is worth a year of ordinary life.

                [*A servant enters and serves coffee.*

Fun. And now for some other information. There are whisperings afloat as to Carson's financial embarrassment, with hints of some crookedness.

Judge. ' I have heard them, but they are not true. They are like the rumors of his engagement to Rose. There was no truth in them. Carson don't want to marry Rose or any other woman. Such men as he don't marry until they are unfit to be the husbands of any women who are fit to be wives—and then a damned fine time they have of it. As to crookedness financially, there need be no fear of that with him. He is a man of scrupulous honor—that way.

Fun. I would not say anything to the contrary—that way; but you must admit that he is leading a life which runs perilously close to the crooked path.

Judge. Yes, but I have no fears that he will overstep it; but if he does and becomes a rascal, he will be one to some purpose, you may depend. He is a bold, strong man. But is it not time that we returned to the house, if we are going to be present at the concert? There is to be some glorious music.

Fan. What is the programme of sports for this evening, Judge?

Judge. There will be the concert first, which was intended to be given here in the garden, but there is a storm approaching, so it will be given in the house. After the concert there will be dancing, which will be kept up until daylight, I suppose.

Fan. There is a very brilliant company assembled, is there not?

Judge. As brilliant and distinguished as could be got together anywhere in America. There is a distinguished leader of Congressional debate, who will be the next President if he don't get cheated out of it; men prominent in literature, commerce, and politics, with their wives and daughters, with many representatives of the local society. There are also some army officers, who served with the Colonel in Mexico, and a live lord.

Fan. A lord! That accounts for the flutter among the gals. I couldn't understand it. It is certain that he is the genuine article?

Judge. Oh, yes; or he wouldn't be here. [*A piano note is heard.*] Ah, there are the first notes of the concert—and here come a few drops of rain. It is time to go in.

> [*Exeunt in the direction of the house. Scene darkens. Faint sounds of distant thunder. Servants enter, who carry out easel and picture.*

ACT III.

Scene—*Evening. Library Parlor, lighted up. Doors at back of scene opening into inner rooms. Rooms right and left. Room on right is so constructed as to give a view within, showing a curtained couch and near it the door of a closet. Music from inner rooms, a sad and plaintive air, during which* Miss Denham *enters and stands in doorway listening for a moment. She then comes forward, seats herself in a chair at a table, leans upon it, despairingly bowing her head upon her hands. Music ceases.*

Miss D., (*rising*). Oh, how my heart, my inmost soul, revolts from the work I have to do—that I must do! There is no escape from it—none but such as I dread more than death itself—the humiliation and disgrace of exposure and the contempt of the one man from whom, of all men in this world, I could the least endure it. Oh, George Marlowe, your contempt would kill me! I cannot tare him from my heart. And the wild hope, born from the words of this man Carson, that if he is separated from Rose I may some day become his wife—shameful as that hope is—I cannot fight against. It has subdued me. Oh, that one fatal mistake of my life! Its consequences follow me like a fate, from which the more I struggle to be free the more I am ensnared.

Enter Carson. *He stands in doorway regarding* Miss Denham.

Car. [*Aside:* And now what has been the result of our interview? I'll venture that the hope of ultimately becoming the wife of Marlowe has brought her to consent.] [*Comes forward.*] And now, that you know the nature of the work you have to do, what is to be your answer? The time is close at hand in which that work is to be done. Come, your answer.

Miss D. Oh, must this work be done, Mr. Carson? Have mercy! Do not force me to do it. For your own sake, give it up. Take some other way to the object you are seeking.

Car. It would be useless. There is no other way; and as there is not, I must go on in this. Rose must be separated from Marlowe. And let me tell you that no such consequences will follow as you imagine. Separated from Marlowe, I can win her,

and within a few months the scandal will be hushed up and regarded as only the indiscretion of a pair of engaged lovers—
nothing more. And within two years you will be free, and with
Marlowe free—I need say no more.

Enter MARLOWE *with* ROSE, *followed by* FANSHAWE *with* MISS DUN-
MORE, JUDGE CROTCHET *with an elderly lady. Some* GUESTS
follow. All seat themselves about the room. DUNMORE *stands in
doorway back. Sounds of storm without.*

Car., (*to Miss D.*) The concert is ended, and the ball-room is
being cleared for dancing, and when it begins it will be time to
attempt our work. I had intended to wait until the guests had
retired, but this storm favors my design, and we will begin now.
Look there! Do you see what is passing between Marlowe and
Rose? What is in Rose's eyes? It is love. The sight of it stirs
the murderous devil within me, and I swear to you if I cannot
rid myself of my rival in no other way I will kill him. Come,
your answer.

Miss D. I must do what you require of me.

Car. That is well. We will begin at once. [*Advancing to*
DUNMORE.] Jack, I am in need of the services of a friend.

Dun. Count me in, John, for anything in that line. When
do you want the shooting to take place?

Car. Oh, it is not a duel. I want this room cleared of everybody except Rose and Miss Denham. Can you do it?

Dun. Easily. I am one of the managers of the ball. I'll go
in and confab with the fiddlers for a reel, and then rush in and
rush everybody off to fill up sets. Will that do?

Car. That will do. Now, go in and arrange for the reel, and
when all is ready come in and stand back in the doorway there
and watch for a signal from me. When I wave my handkerchief rush in and clear the room.

Dun. All right. [*Exit.*

Car., (*to Miss D.*) My plan is now nearly completed; but
Marlowe must be got off the scene by himself. Can you effect it?

Miss D. I will send him away. [*Advances to* MARLOWE.]
George, I have mislaid a bracelet in the conservatory. Will you
kindly search for it?

Mar. I will. [*Exit.*

Car. So! Now for the others.

[DUNMORE *reappears in doorway.* CARSON *waves his handker-*
chief toward him. DUNMORE *turns toward inner rooms and*
waves his handkerchief. A reel strikes up. Then enter
DUNMORE *hurriedly.*

Dun. Come, everybody. The dancing begins. Partners are
wanted to fill up sets for an old-fashioned Virginia reel. Come,
Fanshawe; come, Judge. Partners all.

[*Exeunt into the ball-room all except* ROSE, *who remains seated.*
DUNMORE *reappears in doorway.* CARSON *advances to him.*

Car. Well done, Jack. Now, take out Rose and bring her
back in about five minutes. She will come to meet Marlowe.

Dun., (advancing to Rose). Come, Rose, will you not dance
one set with your cousin?

Rose. With pleasure, John.   [*Exit with* DUNMORE.

Car., (to Miss D.) Dunmore will soon return with Rose, and
when she enters your work will begin. Are you sure that you
understand thoroughly what you will have to do?

Miss D. I am sure.

Car., (pointing to room on R.) That is Rose's room, is it not?

Miss D. It is.

Car. And who occupies the room opposite?

Miss D. That is my room.

Car. And the guests, where will they be lodged?

Miss D. Mostly on the floor above this.

Car. Where will Marlowe sleep?

Miss D. In his studio, on this floor.

Car. In case of any alarm here on this spot during the night,
would it bring him upon the scene?

Miss D. It would. What do you intend concerning him?

Car. No bodily harm, if all goes well. And the same alarm
would bring many of the guests here?

Miss D. Yes.

Car. So, then, the work is arranged. Now, when Dunmore
brings Rose in you must persuade her to retire for the night.
Some means besides persuasion may be necessary. [*Hands*
Miss D. *a small flask.*] Take her into her room, place her upon
that couch, draw the curtains, then withdraw and leave the rest
to me.

Miss D. And look well to what you intend, John Carson. If
that girl does not leave that room with her honor unstained I

will kill you. Do not doubt that I will do it, and know that I am prepared to keep my word. [*Shows dagger.*]

Car. Have no fear. Rose shall come out of that room a pure woman. Bad as I am, I am not mean enough to stain the woman I intend to make my wife.

Re-enter DUNMORE *with* ROSE. *She takes a seat apart.*

Car., (*approaching Dunmore*). Now, Jack, go away, and never hereafter breathe a word of what I have told you concerning Miss Denham or anything concerning her that you may learn here tonight. Promise me this, and the capital for your slave-trading adventure shall not be lacking.

Dun. All right, John; I'll promise anything with that ahead.

Car., (*handing Dunmore a note*). Give this note to Dick Fanshawe. Tell him it is from his father. [*Exit* DUNMORE.

Car., (*to Miss D.*) Now to your work.
[*Retires behind curtain hanging at doorway on R.*

Miss D., (*approaching Rose*). What, Rose, do you not dance?

Rose. Not this set. The places were all taken—and—I don't like a reel.

Miss D. But, Rose, dear, are we not keeping late hours?

Rose. Oh, no!—it is not late. It is not yet twelve.

Miss D. But it is close upon it, dear. And think of what you will have before you tomorrow. There will be the riding party, with the picnic upon the river bank, and dancing again tomorrow night, and you the mistress of it all. You must save your strength, Rose, or you will break down, strong as you are. Let me persuade you to retire.

Rose. Well, I ought to go to bed, really; but those romps of girls in there will not let me. They would hunt the house for me if I should leave them now. And I could not sleep if I went to bed; I am so frightened by this terrible storm.
[*Sounds of storm without.*

Miss D. I can make you sleep, Rose. I have a quieting remedy for excited nerves that I am often obliged to use. Take one little breath of this and you will drop right off to sleep. [*Applies flask to Rose's nostrils.*] Be careful—not too much.

Rose. Why, that does have a quieting effect, truly. I feel sleepy at once. Oh, I must lie down. Don't let—those—girls—find me.

Miss D. They shall not disturb you. Come to your room. I will be your maid for tonight.

[*Miss D. raises* Rose *up. She leans her head on* Miss D.'*s shoulder, who leads her to room on right, places her upon the couch, draws the curtains, and re-enters, meeting* Carson, *who comes forward from behind curtain.*

Miss D. There lies your way, sir.

[*Crosses to room on right, where, through the partly-opened door, she stands looking on.* Dunmore *now reappears at doorway back, peering in.*

Dun. What deep game is my deep friend playing here?

[*Withdraws back as* Carson *approaches.* Carson *pulls together the folding doors leading into the dancing-rooms, closes and locks them. He then turns down the lights, enters* Rose's *room, takes lighted lamp from table on side, goes to the couch, draws the curtain and looks down upon* Rose.

Miss D., (from room opposite). Alas, poor dove, you are in the snare! And I am in the snare. God help me.

[Carson *closes curtain of couch, replaces lamp upon table, turns down the light, goes to closet, which he enters, standing in doorway listening. Knocking is now heard at ball-room doors, with female voices calling, "* Rose! Rose! " *as curtain descends. Storm continues.*

•

ACT IV.—A Year Later.

Scene I—*Apartments of* Fanshawe *and* Marlowe *in New York. Two easels, R. and L., on which are pictures. Other pictures about the room. A Maid Servant dusting.*

Enter Judge Crotchet.

Judge (glancing round). What aerial nook of Bohemia is this that Dick has got himself into, I should like to know? [*Puffs.*] Ten flights of stairs, if it's one.

Maid. Why, the ould loir! It's only foive.

Judge. A studio, eh? Then it is likely that he and Marlowe are together. This girl will know. Young woman, does Mr. Fanshawe live in this house?

Maid. He does, sorr—sometoimes.

Judge. Is he living in it at present?

Maid. I don't know, sorr. I'll go see.

Judge. Well, if he is in and alive, give him this [*handing girl card*], and say that I would like to see him.

Maid. I will, sorr. [*Exit.*

Judge. Marlowe is here. These pictures are evidence enough of that. [*Goes to easel and puts on glasses.*] Ah, a portrait of Miss Denham, and a most marvelous one it is. So, she still lingers upon the scene, does she? I am glad of that. She may be able to throw some light upon the mystery that overhangs Rose. And what is this? [*Turns to other easel.*] A portrait of Rose herself, and a master work it is. What a beastly shame it is that such an artist as Marlowe should remain in obscurity? Ah, Rose, Rose, poor girl, what has become of you? Have the tragic results of that terrible night a year ago led to your death as well as that of your father?

Enter Fanshawe.

Fan. What, Judge Crotchet! Is it possible? [*Shaking hands.*] Well, upon my life, Judge, I am mighty glad to see you. Why, what extraordinary thing can have brought you to this wicked

city? I would not have thought that anything short of oxen
and cart ropes could have done that.

Judge. Well, it is no pleasure excursion that brings me here,
Dick. On the contrary, it is but the beginning of a journey
which, I fear, is destined to end in sorrow and disappointment.

Fan. Why, Judge, what is this?

Judge. It means that I have started out in search of Rose.
The girl has most strangely and mysteriously disappeared, and
under circumstances that lead me to suspect that there has been
foul play.

Fan. Foul play! From whom, in God's name?

Judge. From Rose's southern relatives, the Dunmores of Alabama, and especially from her cousin, John Dunmore.

Fan. What leads you to suspect them?

Judge. Some very ugly circumstances. The first was a letter
written to Rose about nine months ago, shortly after her father's
death, which, as you know, occurred on the night that John
Carson was discovered in Rose's bed-chamber.

Fan. Yes, that I know. But before we come to the matter
of Rose's disappearance, I would like you to give me the full
details of what occurred on that night. I have an especial
reason for asking. While the dancing was going on a note was
put into my hands by Dunmore, who said it was from my father.
The note was a forgery. I found on reaching home that night
that my father knew nothing of it.

Judge. It was a terrible scene that followed your departure.
Some of the young romps of girls when they learned that Rose
had gone to bed determined to go to her room and make her
get up and come back. So off they started. They found the
doors opening from the ball-room closed and locked, but they
managed to get them open and groped their way through the
dark to Rose's sleeping-room, which was also unlighted, but
some one appeared with a light, and then there was a revelation. Rose was found in bed apparently asleep, and on chairs
and on the floor was scattered some male wearing apparel, which
had the appearance of having been left behind in a hurried exit
from the room. At the same moment, attracted by some noise
in the adjoining closet, one of the girls threw open the door.
Then the murder was out. Carson was found there half dressed,
holding down his head in shame. On the instant the voices of

the girls ceased, and a silence followed that was so tragic that many of the guests in the ball-room, becoming alarmed, myself among the number, hurried forward to see what it could mean. We found the girls huddled together, with pale faces. Rose, who had now risen up, and who acted as if half dazed, staggered out into the room among the guests, sank into a chair, and gazed wildly around, letting her eyes rest for a moment on Marlowe, who stood looking at her, and then her head fell forward on her bosom in a manner, as some thought, expressive of the deepest contrition and shame. At this moment the Colonel came in, and at the same moment Carson, as if the devil had sent him, and half dressed as he was, appeared in the doorway of Rose's room. The Colonel seemed very quick to comprehend the meaning of the scene. His face grew white with rage, his eyes flashed, and with the words, "You scoundrel! could you not spare the daughter of your friend?" he seemed as if about to rush upon Carson, at which Miss Denham laid her hand restrainingly upon his shoulder. At this he stopped, clasped his head in his hands, and exclaiming, "My God!" he staggered back and fell to the floor. It was a stroke of apoplexy, brought on by the excitement of the scene. In ten minutes he was a dead man. As her father fell Rose, aroused from what seemed her strange stupor, threw herself with a shriek across her father's body, exclaiming in hysterical cries, "Oh, father! father! father!" The scene was so painful that the guests quit the room, leaving Miss Denham and Rose alone with the body of the Colonel. Carson seemed inclined to stay, but Miss Denham imperiously ordered him off, and he bowed and departed. There was no sleep in the house for any one that night, and the terrible storm that was raging did not lessen the night's horrors. The next day, before ten o'clock, almost every guest had left the house.

Fun. And that same day, I am told, Carson went to Rose and proposed marriage.

Judge. He did. It was the last desperate card in the desperate game he had been playing. He could not wait, for the next day the fact that he had wrecked the bank came out, and that very day he fled the town. In another day his arrest would have followed. Had Rose consented to marry him he might have been saved.

7

Fan. Rose repelled him, I was told by my sister, with such bitter scorn that he actually sneaked out of her presence. That alone was proof of her innocence.

Judge. Yes, to us. But what is the use? The girl's reputation is gone forever.

Fan. I do not think so. There is a hope that the plot against her may yet be revealed—for a plot it certainly was. But now as to Rose's disappearance. The first circumstance connected with it was a letter which you say she received shortly after her father's death?

Judge. That letter was from her cousin, Isabel Dunmore, and was written from Alabama. It was an invitation for Rose to come and spend the winter with her on her plantation near the Florida border. Miss Dunmore wrote that she was ill, and urged Rose to lose no time in coming.

Fan. And Rose accepted that invitation?

Judge. She did, although I did my best in persuading her not to do so; but it was of no use. Belle, she said, was the only friend she had left among women, and she would not remain away from her when she was ill; and so off she started, scarcely taking time enough to make sufficient preparations for the journey.

Fan. And you have heard nothing from her since?

Judge. But once. From Mobile she wrote me a letter, saying that she had been met there by her cousin, John Dunmore, who you know went back to Alabama after the Colonel's death, and that she was to set out with him the next day for the home of Belle.

Fan. It is strange that she should have accepted his escort, knowing the enmity he had for her.

Judge. Perhaps she didn't know it, and perhaps he had dissembled with her as he had done with her father. Anyhow, she accepted his escort and set out with him, and that is the last I have heard of her. I have written to her, to Belle Dunmore herself, and even to the local postmaster, but can get no answer. My belief is that Dunmore has put Rose out of the way—that he has killed her. That, you are aware, would make him the heir to her estate—as he claims.

Fan. It certainly looks ugly. Have you made no other efforts to trace her?

Judge. Yes. After three months, hearing nothing from her, I became alarmed, and securing the shrewdest detective in Rochester, sent him in search of Rose. It was Johnson—you know him. He knew Dunmore, but Dunmore knew nothing of him. In about six weeks I heard from him. He wrote me that he had succeeded in tracing Rose and Dunmore from Mobile to a point within a few miles of Miss Dunmore's plantation, where he lost track of them completely. It was in a wild region, full of blind roads that led nowhere. He kept on until he reached Miss Dunmore's house, where he learned that she was not at home, and that she had been absent ten months. Here his search ended. There was not the faintest clue by which he could trace them further. On his return he made his way to Savannah. Here, one evening, in a gambling saloon, he encountered Dunmore. He got into play with him, and by those methods that detectives know how to use he became intimate with him, and within a week was in his confidence. He learned nothing, however, that would give him any clue to the fate of Rose. One day Dunmore received a letter from New York which contained a draft for a large amount. With this draft he purchased or hired a schooner, and telling Johnson that he was going into the coasting trade, offered him a passage to New York. Johnson accepted. Before the schooner sailed he wrote me an account of his search for Rose, setting the time when the schooner would probably arrive in New York. It arrived day before yesterday. Johnson immediately telegraphed to me, and I lost no time in getting here.

Fan. Your object, I suppose, is to see Dunmore?

Judge. It is. I intend to question him in regard to Rose, assume to believe what he shall say, and then slip quietly away to Alabama and begin my search for her. And, Dick, I am going to take you with me.

Fan. With all my heart, Judge. And if Rose is alive we will find her, and if dead we will trace her murderers and have a revenge as deep as the infernal pit. And now as to one other point. Has it never occurred to you that that letter purporting to be written by Miss Dunmore to Rose might have been a forgery?

Judge. It has occurred to me; but whose forgery?

Fan. That of Dunmore himself.

Judge. Not he. He has not the requisite brains or the education for it. It was a close imitation of Miss Belle's handwriting, and was the work of a person of education.

Fan. He might have had a confederate; and now, Judge, I am going to startle you. It is my opinion that that confederate was John Carson.

Judge. Carson!

Fan. Yes. You know that he and Dunmore left Rochester on the same day, and I am positive that four months later they were together in Alabama.

Judge. That is very important information. But where is Carson now?

Fan. He is not far off—no farther than the room on the floor below this.

Judge. What! Carson in this house?

Fan. Yes; and there is nothing strange in his being here. You know that when I left Rochester I told you that the object I had in doing so was to follow Carson. I had penetrated the object of his plot against Rose, and I felt certain that he would ultimately turn up in New York, that refuge of every played-out scoundrel and adventurer in America. Well, I was not disappointed. One night—it must have been soon after his return from Alabama—I met him in a Broadway gambling-house. Of course we were glad to see each other, and over a bottle we warmed up to our old familiarity. Naturally, we spoke of the past and of that unfortunate affair which had destroyed Rose's reputation. I assumed to believe his explanation of it, that it was unintentional, that he was drunk on that occasion, and that he had done all he could to make reparation, and so forth, and so let the matter drop. Well, I had a part to play. I got tipsy, and so contrived that Carson brought me home. I insisted, in a drunken way, that he should stay all night. To humor me he consented. The next morning I had him to breakfast, and learning from him that he was without money I pressed some upon him as an old friend, and then proposed that he should take a room here in the house at my expense until he could get into funds again. He consented, came that day, and has been here ever since. You know my object in this, Judge?

Judge. Yes; you believe that by keeping near Carson the time will come when he will get into trouble with the law, and that then a confession of his plot against Rose may be extorted from him?

Fan. Yes.

Judge. Oh, that is a wild hope, Dick. Carson is too secretive in character ever to betray himself that way.

Fan. Nevertheless, I shall not give him up; and it is with that hope that Marlowe and I have followed him. He is living on the very verge of crime, and I am not above pushing him into it if the occasion offers. As nearly as I can, I lead the same dissolute life that he does. I gamble with him, get drunk with him, frequent the same haunts, waiting and watching for an opportunity that I believe will some day come. Once in the clutches of the law, he will need friends, and then a confession of his plot against Rose may be bought or extorted from him.

Judge. Dick, you are making a martyr of yourself, and though I cannot think that it will be of any avail, yet I honor you for it. It is your love for Rose, and I wish to God she had married you. ·

Fan. That was not to be. Rose could not bring herself to think of me that way. And the man she does love is my friend, and he is worthy of her. It was something to have saved her from a marriage with Carson. And if I cannot regain the reputation he has stolen from her I will kill him.

Judge. What does Carson do for a living?

Fan. Gambling is his principal source of revenue. He has also a demi-monde connection—a woman who is another man's mistress, and from whom Carson does not disdain to take money. He keeps up a respectable appearance, but in reality he has got down very low.

Judge. Low indeed, if he has got down to living on the wages of a courtesan. Good God, has it come to this with Carson, the one-time social hero of his native city!

Fan. To this complexion has he come.

Judge. And he was once a man of scrupulous honor.

Fan. Honor must have some other anchor than pride, Judge, or it will not hold through such stormy trials as Carson was subjected to. He never had any religious belief.

Judge. True, Dick. Religion is the strong anchor to windward. Is Carson in his room now, do you think?

Fan. No; he is always out at this hour. He will be in at the six o'clock dinner. And you may be certain that Dunmore will be in his company. And if you will stay to dinner, Judge, you will meet another acquaintance of yours whom I am sure you will be glad to see—Miss Denham.

Judge. Miss Denham! What! is she here, too?

Fan. She is; and that is also easily accounted for. This house was her New York home before she went on her theatrical tour. Marlowe also lived here at that time. On their return they naturally came back to it. And Marlowe coming here, I naturally came with him.

Judge. So, that accounts for you all being in the same house, eh? The dramatic cohesion is strong. Is Miss Denham friendly with Carson?

Fan. She seems to be, though she knows positively nothing of his way of life. The part he plays with her is that of a remorseful and repentant man, and as Miss Denham is naturally a generous and forgiving woman, he seems to do it successfully. I greatly fear, however, that he has some design upon her fortune. She seems to have a small one. In fact, I know that he has already engaged her in a speculation of some kind, though what it is I cannot imagine.

Judge. As to her fortune, I can tell you something to the woman's credit. It consisted of diamonds given to her by the Colonel. After his death she went to Rose and offered to return them. Rose insisted that she should keep them.

Fan. She is certainly an honorable woman.

Judge. Does she take the Colonel's death much to heart?

Fan. It may be. There is something preying on her mind. Seemingly, the only thing that gives her interest in life is her ambition for making Marlowe known to the world for the great artist he is. That seems to have become a passion with her. She has one of those rare minds that understand art.

Judge. It is a dirty shame that such an artist as Marlowe can find no recognition in his own country. And what a comment on our democracy it is! An artist who is not unworthy to wear the mantle of Hogarth sinks into neglect and obscurity, while the hero of a prize ring can hold a reception in the Senate chamber. Well, there has been enough said upon that subject. And now, Dick, come with me to my hotel round the corner. Johnson is there, and I want to see him before I meet Dunmore.

Fun. Very good. I will leave a note for Marlowe, telling him to send for us if Dunmore and Carson should come in during our absence.

[*Sits down and writes note, leaving it on table. Exeunt, R.*

Enter MARLOWE, L. *He lays aside a portfolio that he brings in, takes up note and reads it, then sits down at easel and begins work. Then enter* MISS DENHAM, *reading.*

Miss D. What, George, returned? I thought your studio was deserted, and came here to read. I like this place to read in. It is so quiet always—and if I tire of my book I can turn to your work and read there what never tires.

Mar. Indeed! And what do you find in my work that is so especially interesting?

Miss D. Human nature—human life—what it is that life and time and passion write in human faces.

Mar. I think you have too high an estimate of my work, Aliena.

Miss D. Indeed I do not.

Mar. Well, then, here is more reading for you—since you like it so well.   [*Handing her portfolio.*

Miss D. More comedies and tragedies from the streets, I suppose—from bar-rooms, from hotel corridors, and from the haunts of Circe—something to laugh over, to think over, and to weep over. Ah, art fulfills her true function in your work, George. And what a lesson is taught in these sketches here! If it could be brought to the eyes of those who need it, many a lost one might be turned from the path that leads to perdition. Here in this first sketch, where prostitution is so luxuriously veiled as to be scarcely suspected, to these others, that lead one by a gradual descent through the vilest haunts of the city, where the features of Circe are so hideous as to be sickening, you portray one face through them all, that of a young girl, following her to the last scene of all, a midnight leap from the dock to a death in the river. Ah, what a lesson it teaches! It makes me shudder. Ah, how faithfully does pencil hold the mirror up to life! And yet you are unknown.

Mar. Yes, and most likely to remain so.

Miss D. You shall not remain so. You shall yet come forth from this obscurity that surrounds you. To that work I have devoted my life, and I will accomplish it. What is wanting to bring you to the recognition of the world but the power that wealth gives?

Mar. But that is a power that you have not.

Miss D. True, I have it not, as yet. But it is a power that I shall have, and the time is not far distant. Even now Fortune is holding out her hand to me and tempting me with a scheme of adventure in which there is the promise—nay, the certainty—of wealth beyond my wildest hopes.

Mar. Indeed! Then you had best take hold of Fortune's hand and lose no time about it. She is a fickle goddess.

Miss D. I intend to—or think I shall. I have only been waiting to know what a dear friend of mine may think of the adventure. Now, George, what do you think of the slave trade?

Mar. The slave trade. Well, I can't say that I have a very high opinion of that.

Miss D. Ah, I knew you would condemn it. But did you never think how much of the popular feeling against it is due to prejudice, not to say ignorance? I once held it in utter detestation, but reflection and later knowledge have made me regard it with quite different eyes.

Mar. It is a matter of reason and conscience alone, Aliena. If they do not condemn, you need not hesitate. "There is nothing either good or bad but thinking makes it so." Such is the testimony of Shakespeare.

Miss D. It is not bad in my thinking. I can see in it something that far outweighs the evil—the design of Providence for the spread of civilization in regions now in the darkness of barbarism.

Mar. There is some soul of goodness in things evil. There is more of Shakespeare for you. And so it is a slave-trading adventure that you propose to invest some money in, I suppose.

Miss D. It is.

Mar. Well, it is a trade that is carried on extensively, though secretly, from this port. Many a colossal fortune has been built up from the profits of it by men who own pews in churches.

Miss D. Then my mind is made up. I shall hesitate no longer, but depart at once. Tomorrow you may not find me here, George.

Mar. Indeed! Is it your intention to take a personal part in the adventure?

Miss D. Oh, no! [*Laughing.*] I am not going to sail for the coast of Africa. I am only going to Florida, to be near the scene of the enterprise, and do my best to see that it is conducted on the most humane principles. In two years I shall return here. And then I shall be no longer the poor music teacher, but rich, and then—America shall know her artist.

Mar. Do not be too sanguine. And do you really go to-morrow ?

Miss D. Tomorrow certainly; and perhaps tonight. Everything is ready and waiting for me to go on board, I am told. And now, George, as there is a possibility that I may never return, there is something that I want you to promise me. Here is the key of a writing desk that I will leave with you. At the end of two years, if I do not return and you do not hear from me, you may be certain that I am no longer living. Then unlock the desk. You will find a sealed paper addressed to you. Read it. Do you promise me ?

Mar. I do. [*Aside:* Some one is entering Carson's room below. Perhaps he and Dunmore have come in. I must know.] [*Exit.*

Miss D. The sad and bitter story of my life he will find written in that paper, and he will read there what I had not the strength to reveal while living, and when I shall be beyond the sound of all earthly reproach.

Re-enter MARLOWE.

Mar. [*Aside:* Dunmore and Carson are below. Dick and the Judge must know of it at once.] And now, Aliena, I am called away. As you go away so soon I may not find you here on my return.

Miss D. Then let us say good-bye now.

[*She takes his hand and they go toward the door. Part way she stops, leans her head upon his shoulder, and gives way to tears.*

Mar. Come, come, Aliena, my brave girl, this is not like you. We are not parting never to meet again. We shall meet again, never doubt it, and all shall be well. Good-bye. [*Exit.*

Miss D. Farewell! farewell! and forever farewell to the only hope that has sustained me through so many bitter trials— through so much suffering and remorse, a hope for which I have

8

sacrificed almost my hopes of heaven itself. I cannot give him up—my heart will cling to him even in despair. [*Turns to the portrait of* ROSE.] Here is the face that he loves. Oh, Rose! Rose! with what reproach you seem to look upon me. Oh, God! is there not some way of making reparation to this girl, of restoring to her the reputation I have aided in stealing from her without sinking so low in the esteem of the man I love?—some way of ending this long heartache and remorse? No, there is no way. I could not endure his contempt, his scorn. I must suffer to the end—give my life to the only reparation I can make to him—and then die.

[*Sinks into a chair at the foot of the portrait, leans forward, and buries her face in her hands. Then enter* CARSON. *He walks aside and stands regarding her.*

Car. [*Aside:* Parting from Marlowe, it seems. Strange how she clings to that fellow when she must know that she is but cherishing a hopeless passion. But it seems ever the fate of these women who sway all hearts to love some one man hopelessly. Well, so much the better—in this case. She will now make Dunmore happy by going to Florida.

Miss D., (*rising*). Pardon me, Mr. Carson, I did not see you. You have come, I suppose, for my answer to Captain Dunmore's invitation. I have decided to accept it.

Car. You will not regret it. The climate will restore your health, and you will find every comfort awaiting you at his rendezvous. The Captain is in my room below. Will you see him?

Miss D. Not today. I have many preparations to make. I shall meet him tomorrow on board his vessel.

Car. It has been arranged to have you go aboard tonight. It is best to lose no time. A carriage will take you to a hotel near the Battery, where the Captain and I will meet you and take you on board.

Miss D. Very good.

Car. There is not the slightest obstacle in the way of our success, Miss Denham. The enterprise will pay enormous profits, it will be conducted on the most humane principles, and you shall return with your investment increased to a million.

Miss D. I shall owe you a great debt, sir.

Car. You will owe me nothing. It will be but a slight return for the generosity of your forgiveness for the great wrong I have done you.

Miss D. Say no more of that, sir. I have learned to regard the wrong you speak of as but the consequences of a fate that ensnared us both, and we are now seeking in the conduct of our lives to make such atonement as we can. [*Exit.*

Car. Yes, that is what you are doing—treading the path that leads to the heaven you believe in. As for me, I seem to be going in the other direction. Well, both roads meet at the same terminus, I'm thinking—over the brink of the grave into the abyss of nothingness. And so believing, why should I not be the man I am?

Enter DUNMORE.

Car. Ah, Jack, you are here, eh? Couldn't wait, eh? Must see your charmer? Well, you will have to wait until you see her on board tomorrow.

Dun. And so she has consented to go to Florida, has she? And I haven't come all the way from Savannah for nothing—for it is on her account that I have come.

Car. Well, you will have a chance for your wooing now. [*Aside:* But it is mighty little good it will do you, I'm thinking.]

Dun. And so she has consented to become a partner with us, eh? That suggestion I made to you up there at the Colonel's was a good idea, John.

Car. It was.

Dun. Did you have any trouble in bringing her to consent?

Car. I did. At first she would not hear of it; actually revolted at the idea; but I showed her how by the money she could make in the trade she would have it in her power to make Marlowe known to the world. That caught her. A few days thereafter she consented to advance the capital we wanted, and gave me that draft which I sent to you at Savannah. And now she will argue a minister out of his pulpit on the subject of the slave trade. [*They laugh.*] And now sit down. I want to hear how your scheme for getting possession of the Vaughn estate is getting on.

Dun. It is getting on splendidly, though not exactly as I calculated in the legal way, yet it is going on all right in another way. In about a year I calculate that the principal obstacle will be removed. Then the estate will be mine, and you will be half a million richer. That decoy letter that you wrote, John, was a trump card. It is going to win.

Car. So Rose did go South in answer to it, eh?

Dun. She did; and she went somewhat farther south than she expected; and her journey isn't ended yet.

Car. Well, go ahead, but be cautious. Don't tell me anything more. I am afraid, Jack, that you are a little too reckless. And now, how long before we are to go on board?

Dun. Tomorrow, I hope, though I am not certain. I lack a few sailors yet, which I expect my mate will capture tonight in a shanghaeing den.

Car. In a shanghaeing den, eh?

Dun. Yes; but that will be an easy job. But there is one thing I want mighty bad, John, and can't get. I want a good doctor.

Car. Can't you get one?

Dun. Not one that is good for anything. I can get a swab that calls himself a doctor, but he don't know as much of medicine as a loblolly boy. Sometimes on these voyages one-half the niggers die and have to be tossed to the sharks. A good doctor on board would prevent all that.

Car. Then we must certainly have a doctor. I might be tossed to the sharks myself, and so might you.

Dun. But how are we to get one?

Car. Shanghae one, as you propose to do with some of your crew.

Dun. You are joking; but that is what I'd do mighty quick if I could get the chance.

Car. The chance is easily got, it seems to me. Get up a case of sickness in that shanghaeing den you speak of, call a doctor in and nab him.

Dun. A good idea; and if you know a doctor who could be got into one of those dens without a platoon of police to protect him, we'll try it on.

Car. I don't know a doctor in the whole city, except Dick Fanshawe, and he is not in practice.

Dun. And a mighty good doctor he is, as I happen to know. He saved my life once, after that cutting I got in a Rochester den. But he is too wide awake to be got into a shanghaeing den.

Car. I think it might be done. Dick is dare-devil enough to go anywhere.

Dun. But, then, John, it would be playing a low-down game on a friend.

Car. Oh, Dick would soon get over that. He is a reckless, devil-may-care Bohemian, and would soon come around. You could rate him for high pay, and so smooth the matter over.

Dun. I could rate him for pay so high that it would make him a rich man inside of two years. By the gods, John, we'll try this, if you say so.

Car. I am agreed, Jack. We must have a doctor. That's a sine qua non.

Dun. Then it is settled. And now, how is Fanshawe to be got into that den?

Car. That will be easy enough. We will invite him to a supper at Pfaff's. After that take him for a stroll along the docks. He'll go. He is very fond of a spree in my company. And then we can easily conduct him into that shanghaeing den where you are going to nab your sailors.

Dun. And once in there he is caught. A little drugged liquor will fix him, and the next thing he knows he will find himself under hatches and well out to sea. When will Fanshawe come in?

Car. At the dinner hour, which is not far off. Sit down and have a cigar.

Dun. No; I will go down and see the landlady. I want to know if she got the fruit I sent her.　　　　　　*[Exit.*

Car. So, then, Rose did go to Alabama, and was entrapped by Dunmore, eh? Well, she must now go to whatever fate Dunmore has in store for her. I know not what he intends, and it is too late to interfere if I did. Good God! to think that I could take part in a plot against a woman I once wanted to make my wife! And I a man once so proud of my honor that I would have killed a man who would have impugned it! That episode of forgery, embezzlement, and conspiracy, and the subsequent life into which I lapsed seems to have completely transformed me. Is it the sensual life I have led, or is it the gambling passion that possesses me—that passion that swallows up honor' pride, and conscience—that has wrought this change in me? Perhaps. If I were superstitious I could easily believe in a supernatural retribution that has seems to have followed me from the day I plotted against poor Doughton. The money I

gained in that scheme I invested in a speculation that swept
away my entire fortune. That led to forgery and embezzlement; that to a conspiracy against my friend and his daughter; and now here I am, almost at the bottom of the hill in my
descent to Avernus, down which I have followed by always
seeing ahead of me a way of escape. Well, what is the next
step in the dark way? What is to come in this slave-trading
adventure? Is it to be the same fateful sequence? It is full of
peril. Something says pause, but there is something stronger
still that urges me on. [*Street door-bell rings below.*] That must
be Dick. [*Opens door and listens.*] Yes; it is he and Marlowe.
And who is this coming up with them? Judge Crotchet, as I
live! [*Steps back.*] So, more hypocrisy.

Enter FANSHAWE, JUDGE CROTCHET, *and* MARLOWE.

Judge. What, Carson! Why, John, is this really you?

Car. Yes, Judge. Or the man who was once John Carson.

Judge. Well, upon my life, John, I am glad to see you.

Car. I am glad to hear you say so, Judge. It is more than
I would have had any right to expect.

Judge. Well, John, there was a time when I felt a little cantankerous toward you, but it was because you ran away. Why
didn't you stay and let your friends pull you through? They
would have done it. [*Aside:* That is on the raw, I think.]

Car. So I have learned since, Judge. But you know the old
adage, the wicked fly when no man pursueth; and thus conscience doth make cowards of us all. But there was something
I could not fly from—remorse and the memories of the past.
For the past year I have endured the torments of the damned.

Judge. Upon my life, John, I feel for you. Let us sit down
and talk matters over.   [*They retire back.*

Re-enter DUNMORE.

Dun. What, Fanshawe, old man, are you alive yet? Tip us
your flipper, my hearty.   [*They shake hands.*

Fan. Glad to see you, Dunmore. Why, I was beginning to
think you had been washed under, you are so long overdue.

Dun. Well, you see I've been knocking about the Southern
coast in chase of a schooner I used to own. I've got her at last,
and now it is no longer the tar and turpentine lay, but ebony

and ivory. How d' do, Mr. Marlowe? Hope I see you well, sir.

Mar. Quite well, thank you, Captain.

[DUNMORE *sees the* JUDGE *and strikes a comic sailor attitude of surprise.*

Dun. Well, dash my toplights if there isn't Judge Crotchet! How d' do, Judge?

Judge, (*coldly*). How do you do, Dunmore?

Dun. Glad to see you, Judge. Though we parted in something of a miff, I hope there is no cantankerous feeling——

Judge. Not on my part. Those missing papers that disappeared from the safe on the night of your uncle's death did not complicate matters much.

Dun. Those missing papers, eh? So you still think 1 took them, do you?

Judge. It is no matter what I think about it. Rose holds the estate as her father's heir, and if you or any of your relatives think she does not, just try to get it, that's all.

Dun. Brag is a good dog, Judge.

Judge. Holdfast is a good one too.

Dun. Well, avast, Judge. You are ahead of us on the law tack, as matters stand at present, so we won't discuss the subject now. How is Rose?

Judge. You can best answer that question. You have seen her since I have.

Dun. I haven't seen her since her father's funeral, a year ago.

Judge. You have not? Did you not meet her in Mobile and conduct her to her cousin Belle's plantation four months ago?

Dun. It is not likely, since I have not been in Mobile for the past two years.

Judge. She wrote to me that she had met you there.

Dun. Then she wrote what was not true. But I think I can explain the matter. There is another John Dunmore down there, a first cousin to Belle and a second cousin to me, and it was probably him she met.

Judge. H'm! Perhaps. I didn't know of No. 2.

Dun. You see, Judge, the Dunmores are so numerous down there that they use up all the Christian names and sometimes have to double up on one. And so Rose went South to see Belle, did she?

Judge. She did. And it is very strange that I can't hear from her. I am afraid something has happened to her.

Dun. I reckon not, Judge. She and Belle are doubtless gallivanting about the State somewhere, visiting relatives. There is no end to the Vaughns and Dunmores down there, and post-offices don't exist where some of them live. I reckon Rose is all right.

Judge. I hope so.

Dun. Though I must admit that there are Dunmores down there who would not scruple to put her out of her misery if she came their way. You know what I refer to.

Judge. I do. But her father is dead and gone to his account. What revenge would it be to strike his innocent daughter?

Dun. Not any for me. But there are Dunmores down there who are not so forgiving, who were engaged in the old vendetta, and who took an oath that not a member of the Colonel's family should be left alive.

Judge. Yes; and that makes it mighty strange that Belle should have invited Rose down there among so many enemies.

Dun. It was rather queer. But I reckon she thought she would be able to keep Rose out of harm's way.

Judge. I hope she will be able to do it.   [*Retires back.*

Dun. [*Aside:* The old duffer evidently suspects something, but I reckon I've bamboozled him on to the wrong scent. But how is his arrival going to stand in with our game to nab Fanshawe? [*Approaches* CARSON.] See here, John, is the coming of the Judge going to interfere with our scheme?

Car. It will not interfere. We will have to take the Judge and Marlowe along after supper. They are not to be separated now; and once on the ground you can easily pilot them into your shanghaeing den. Can you separate them there, take Fanshawe and leave the Judge and Marlowe behind?

Dun. Easily.

Car. Then the work is done. And now I will arrange the programme for carrying it out. [*Approaches the Judge.*] Judge, I hope you intend to make something of a stay in town.

Judge. Only for a day or two, John. As soon as I have finished the business that brought me here I am off.

Car. Well, while you do remain you must let Dick and I do the honors and show you some of the sights of the town.

Judge. Well, John—— [FANSHAWE *nudges the* JUDGE *to accept.*] Well, John, you know I am fond of being amused, and I shall want something to tell the family.

Car. Well, then, what do you say for a visit to the theatre after supper? We will make up a party and go and see the great Charlotte in Old Meg, and after that we will have a quiet midnight stroll along the docks. Dick and Marlowe shall show us some of their Hogarthian localities.

Judge. Very good, John. I shall be glad to have a look at them.

Car. So! Then it is arranged. You shall have dinner with us here. [*Bell rings below.*] And it is already served. [*To* DUN-MORE: Now, Jack, go down to that den of yours and get everything ready. I will be there with Dick, the Judge, and Marlowe within an hour. After supper it will be too late to go to the theatre, and we will leave here and go direct to your den.

Dun. All right, John. I will lay off for you in the region of Fulton market. Now, gentlemen [*going*], I regret to say that urgent business compels me to leave you. I will meet you after the theatre, however, and join in the fun that will follow.

[*Exit. Then exeunt* FANSHAWE, CARSON, *the* JUDGE, *and* MARLOWE.

[At the end of this scene the curtain falls for a few minutes.]

SCENE II—*The Interior of a Water Street dance-house. A long, low room. On left a bar, behind which stands Bartender. On right, benches and barrels. On a barrel is seated a fiddler. A mixed collection of women, sailors, negroes, and dock-loafers. Enter, from door on left, in front,* DUNMORE, CARSON, FANSHAWE, JUDGE CROTCHET, *and* MARLOWE.

Dun. Now, boys, keep together and let the women alone, and you are all right; and don't drink anything but such as you see me drink. [*Goes back and converses with bartender.*

Fan. Well, Judge, here you are in a Water street dance-house. How do you like the looks of it?

Judge. I don't like the looks of it at all, Dick; and I'm damned if I don't feel a little nervous. My God! what a scene! I wish my wife could see this. It would cure her of ever giving more money to foreign missions.

9

Fan. Now you are talking, Judge. Here is the true missionary field—here under the very shadow of the church steeples.

Judge. Then why don't they come here and work it?

Fan. They will, perhaps, when they get done quarreling with the theatre and settling points of doctrine.

Judge. Now you are talking, Dick.

[DUNMORE *comes back and joins* CARSON *and the others.*

Judge. Look at that fiddler over there on that whisky barrel. Did you ever see a more perfect likeness of the stage Mephistopheles?

Fan., (*laughing*). I never did. And he is quite apropos to the place. It is the devil's music that is danced to here.

Dun. I know the man, Judge. It is his fancy to get himself up that way, and a devilish good fellow he is. [*To* CARSON: That is my mate, Jones. I'll go over and give him his instructions. In half an hour the job will be done. [*Crosses over to* JONES: Look here, Jones, do you see that good-looking, square-shouldered chap over there in the shooting coat and felt hat? That is the man we want. That is the doctor.

Jones. All right, Captain. There will be a dance; after that give me the signal, and in ten minutes he will be behind the panel, and an hour later he will be on board.

Dun. Make no mistake now. Take him and the three sailors I pointed out to you and no one else. And mind you, let the bottle alone until your work is done. If you don't, damme, I'll put you under hatches until we reach the coast.

Jones. Have no fears, Captain. I'll not touch a drop.

Dun. Very good. After the dance send that girl to me. [*Indicating one of the women.*] She knows what to do.

[*Rejoins* CARSON *and others.*

Dun. Now, gentlemen, what sort of entertainment will you have? Acrobatic, burnt cork, opera bouffe, jimcrackeric unlimited, sailor's hornpipe, topic song—what shall it be? There is plenty of talent in the company, specially engaged for this occasion.

Fan. Don't give us anything of that sort, Dunmore. If it should please the crowd, a half dozen handclappers would keep it going for an hour. The Judge wants to get away.

Dun. Well, then, we'll have a dance to wind up with and then go.   [*Raises his hand as a signal to* JONES.

Jones, (shouting). Gentlemen, take partners for a dance.

[*Strikes up a tune. A grotesque dance follows. After the dance one of the women approaches* DUNMORE.

Woman. Come, Cap, what is it going to be? I 'spose you know the rules of the shebang.

Dun. No, my beauty. [*Chucking her chin.*] What are the rules of the shebang?

Woman. It's treat, trade, or travel; and there ain't a going to be no let up on 'em, you bet. This ain't no church picnic.

Dun. Well, we'll treat, and travel afterwards. Come, boys, let us give the gals a drink and then get away. [*Aside to* CARSON: Now the trap is about to spring. The fight will be a put-up job. Don't get mixed up in the scrimmage, or they'll dose you.

[DUNMORE, FANSHAWE, CARSON, MARLOWE, *and the* JUDGE *approach the bar, led by the woman. Liquor is set out. Men and women crowd up and drink.* DUNMORE *lays bill on counter.* BARTENDER *puts bill in drawer, returning no change.*

Dun. Look, here, you bullet-headed shark, what do you mean? I don't pay for all this crowd.

Bartender. Yez do pay for them.

Dun. I'm damned if I do. It's only drinks for the women I pay for.

Fan. For God's sake, Dunmore, don't quarrel here. It would be as much as our lives are worth. Let him keep the bill.

Dun. I'm damned if I do. Give me my change, you slush-eating swab, or I'll cave your lights in.

Bartender. Fwhat's that? Ye'll cave my lights in, will yez? Begorra, ye're just the man I'm looking for.

[*Leaps over the counter and attacks* FANSHAWE, *who knocks him down. At this the crowd yell and a general fight begins.* DUNMORE *and* CARSON *step one side.* FANSHAWE *shouts:* "Strike out, boys, and make for the door." *He,* MAR-LOWE, *the* JUDGE, *and three sailors are crowded back against the wall in rear of room, where a panel opens, through which they are pushed. Some of the crowd make an attempt at rescue.* DUNMORE, *standing at entrance of panel, holds them back with raised pistol.*

ACT V.—TEN DAYS LATER.

SCENE I—DUNMORE'S *slave-trading rendezvous on the coast of Florida. On left an old plantation house, with veranda, which projects into a garden, in which are branching oaks, palmetto trees, and shrubbery. The scene is apparently on the verge of a plateau, which slopes gently down to a wide lagoon, in which, inshore, on right, rising above the trees, are seen the masts of a schooner. Looking across the lagoon, the view stretches away over a tropic swamp until it catches a far-off glimpse of an island-studded bay which sets in from the sea.*

Enter FANSHAWE *and* MARLOWE, *who come apparently from the schooner.*

Fan., (*looking around*). So, here we are at last, are we, in the pirate's home, the slave-trader's rendezvous?

Mar. And a most enchanting spot it is—a veritable paradise, so far as scenery goes.

Fan. And so here it is that Dunmore will land his wild Africans, is it? Quite a romantic sequel to our adventure in a Water street dance-house of ten days ago, is it not?

Mar. It is; and a sequel that I would think more character-istic of the days of Kidd than of these peaceful commercial days of 1857.

Fan. It is just as characteristic of these days, my boy, as of the days of Kidd and his pirates. New York is and has been for a hundred years and more the secret fitting-out place for slavers; and as for the kidnapping of crews, that is and has been an every-day occurrence. And if Dunmore kidnapped a sailor, why should he not kidnap a doctor, if he wanted one and could get him in no other way?

Mar. Yes; that I can understand; but why should he kidnap an artist and a lawyer? To what possible use can he put me and the Judge?

Fan. You and the Judge were taken by mistake, and con-trary to Dunmore's orders. After the fight in that Water street den, and after we were shoved behind the panel and chloro-formed, Dunmore and Carson left the place, leaving the rest of

:he work to be done by that old pirate, his mate. The mate got drunk and confused his orders, with the result that you and the Judge were brought aboard the schooner along with me and three sailors. Dunmore did not discover the mistake until the next morning, when he came to take a look at me in the hold. The schooner was then well out to sea, and rough weather setting in, it was too late to set you ashore. Such is the statement I get from Carson. I have not had a chance to speak with Dunmore as yet, the voyage has been so rough, and he has seemingly kept out of my way.

Mar. Well, I suppose we must make up our minds for a voyage to the African coast.

Fan. Possibly, though we need be in no hurry about it.

Mar. What do you mean?

Fan. I mean that we may find some means of escape before the schooner sails.

Mar. Not much hope of that. Dunmore will doubtless suspect some such attempt and will watch us closely.

Fan. Yes; most likely. But I think I can find a way of putting his vigilance to sleep, and perhaps put him to sleep and all his crew.

Mar. Indeed! How would you do that!

Fan. By means of a very powerful opiate that I have found in the schooner's medicine chest. With that I propose to drug some of the liquor, of which the schooner carries a large supply. By watching my chance, I think I can so manage as to get Dunmore and all hands to take a drink with me at a favorable time. If they do that they will sink into a stupor that will last long enough to carry out my design. Dunmore will wake to find his schooner burned to the water's edge, his boats stove, and his prisoners beyond his reach. My novel-writing taste has made me fruitful in expedients.

Mar. It is a scheme that might succeed.

Fan. And I have already made a discovery that will aid me greatly in carrying it out. I have discovered a brother among the crew.

Mar. What! a brother among the crew! Is it possible?

Fan. Yes; a brother—Mason.

Mar. Oh!

Fan. I am a member of the order, you must know. On the

voyage down it occurred to me that there might be some Masons among the crew. I made signals, and sure enough, one popped up. He proved to be one of the three sailors who were captured with us. If I need any help he will come to my aid, you may be certain.

Mar. But why does Dunmore come here? Why did he not sail for the coast of Africa direct from New York?

Fan. He comes here for some kind of a cargo, so I am informed by Carson, though what it is is more than I can imagine.

Mar. Perhaps it is something that he has got stored in that negro cabin that you can see in that grove of oaks and palmettoes yonder [*pointing*], with an armed sailor on guard before the door.

Fan. I see the grove, but no cabin and no sailor. Ah, yes; I see them now, very dimly, through the trees. Well, it may be. He has evidently got something there that he is very careful of, and apparently very much afraid that somebody will see. And the cabin window boarded up, too.

Mar. And I wonder if what he has there had anything to do with his mysterious visit ashore last night after the schooner arrived in the lagoon.

Fan. Possibly. And so you saw that, too, did you? I saw that myself. For two hours I lay awake, watching through a porthole of the schooner the gleaming of mysterious lights through the old mansion here and among the trees, being carried back and forth apparently between the house and that cabin. And it is a circumstance that has put a strange and most painful fancy into my novel-writing head.

Mar. Indeed! What is it?

Fan. Never mind now. It might be paining you needlessly. Wait until I look into the secret that is locked up in that cabin.

Mar. Don't you think it best not to meddle with it?

Fan. I do not. Secrets are very attractive to me, and I am of a very meddlesome disposition, anyhow.

Enter DUNMORE, *followed by the crew, who carry casks, baskets, guns, oars, and coils of rope. Then enter* CARSON, MISS DENHAM, JUDGE CROTCHET, *and* OLD DAN, *who carries shawls and portmanteau.* JONES *follows, with a patch over his eye. An old negro woman and a mulatto girl come out of the house.*

Dun., (*to crew*). Lay the things on the veranda there. [*Crew deposit casks, oars, &c., on the veranda.*] We will stow them when everything is ashore. Stand those rifles against that tree. So! Now put those cases of liquor at the other end of the veranda. That will do. Now cover them with that tarpaulin.

Fan., (*to Marlowe*). Dunmore don't think it safe, apparently, to leave the liquor and arms on board. Well, so much the better for the object I have in view. Those cases of brandy are just handy. [*Exeunt crew.*

Dun., (*coming forward*). Well, gentlemen, here we are at last, after a very stormy passage, safe in what you would call the pirate's home, I suppose, Fanshawe. Well, I hope you like the looks of it.

Fan. It is a most enchanting spot, Dunmore.

Dun. And how do you like it, Mr. Marlowe?

Mar. I find it in every way delightful, Captain.

Dun. I am glad you like the place, sir, and sorry that it is not in accordance with my plans to have you stay here through the winter. You and the Judge were taken by mistake, which I suppose has been explained to you. It was only Fanshawe I wanted.

Fan., (*to Marlowe*). And I reckon he will prove a Tartar before you have done with him.

Mar., (*to Fan.*) Now, Dick, you are going to quarrel with him. For God's sake, don't do that. He has the temper of a tiger, and he might kill you.

Fan. Never fear. I know how to tame a tiger. There will be a method in my madness, and I will turn the quarrel to good account. Besides, I must vent my overflowing gall. I must tell him to his teeth my opinion of the dirty trick he has played upon us. [*To* DUNMORE: Captain, you just remarked to Mr. Marlowe that it was only me you wanted for this voyage.

Dun. Only you, Dick. You see I was obliged to have a doctor, and as I could get one in no other way I took you, trusting that I could make it all right with you finally. It was a rough deal on a friend, but I couldn't help myself.

Fan. A rough deal, you call it. Yes, it was all that, and as dirty a trick as ever was played upon a man under the guise of friendship.

Dun. What, Fanshawe! [*Laying his hand upon his knife.*] Have a care. This is not language to use to me now.

Fan. I repeat what I say, Dunmore, and add that it was not only the act of a villain, but the act of a mean villain.

[*The* JUDGE, *who has been walking moodily up and down, pauses and becomes interested.*

Dun. By the gods, Fanshawe!

[*Drawing his knife.* FANSHAWE *stands unmoved.* CARSON *comes forward and grasps* DUNMORE'S *hand.* MISS DENHAM *comes forward.*

Miss D. Gentlemen, for heaven's sake, don't quarrel.

Fan. Not while you are present, Miss Denham.

Miss D. Mr. Fanshawe, will you hear a few words that I wish to say?

Fan. Assuredly, Miss Denham.

Miss D. In what I have to say, sir, I shall not attempt to excuse the treatment you have received. I knew nothing of the design to entrap you, and had I known of it I would have had nothing to do with this voyage until that design had been given up. Do you believe me, sir?

Fan. I do, most positively.

Miss D. I thank you, sir. And now let me add a few words of personal explanation. You doubtless think it strange to find me here engaged in this enterprise. I can see no wrong in it. To me the slave traffic seems the process of social evolution—the bringing of lower races in contact with higher. I think God's hand is in it. Some day there will be a backward flow of freed and Christianized slaves from this continent, and then civilization and religion will be planted in regions now in the darkness of savagery and barbarism. I do believe it, sir.

Fan. [*Aside:* Ah, how beautifully this plays into my hands! And now for a bold card in the game.] Upon my life, Miss Denham, I am deeply impressed by what you say. You place the slave traffic before me in a new light. I had not thought of regarding it from this point of view.

Miss D. Can you not regard it as the correct view?

Fan. I can—and do from this moment. [*Aside:* God forgive me!]

Miss D. Then, sir, why can you not take the position of surgeon on yonder vessel, if by your skill you could save hundreds of poor wretches from disease and death and for contact with a higher life?

Fan. I can take that position, Miss Denham—can regard it as a duty—and in that spirit I accept it. Captain Dunmore, I will be your surgeon, if it suits you. And here let me retract the rough words I used to you. John, I ask your pardon.

[CARSON *turns away with a shrug of indifference.*

Dun. Never mind the rough words you used to me, Fanshawe. I make allowances for a good deal of rough lingo when I come across a man in a foul way, as I did you. But I don't mean to carry it out that way. After a few voyages I intend to set you ashore a rich man. Besides, you are a plucky one, and that's the kind of man I like. It did me good to see the way you tumbled some of the swabs in that den where I took you. You gave my mate Jones an eye that will last him the voyage. He will need your services. I will make you better acquainted. Mr. Jones, this way, if you please. [JONES *comes forward.*] Jones, give the doctor a glimpse of that starboard blinker of yours that he closed up so beautifully the other night.

[JONES *lifts the patch over his eye.*

Fan. Well, that must have been a blow, indeed. Did you get it from me?

Jones. I did, sir, and it lifted me right off my feet, sir.

Dun. Knocked out in the first round. But he bears you no malice, doctor. Do you, Jones?

Jones. Not in the least, Captain. It is what we look for on such occasions.

Dun. Jones, the doctor is a book writer. Maybe he'll write your life.

Fan. I should certainly be pleased to be the biographer of so remarkable a navigator as Mr. Jones seems to be.

[*Salutes* JONES, *who bows low.*

Dun. Now, Mr. Jones, you can get the crew together here in the garden. I have a few words to say to them, and I reckon I'll say it now. [*Exit* JONES.

Fan., (*to* MARLOWE, *as they walk aside*). The quarrel was a bold card, but it seems to have won. Dunmore will have no suspicion now that we intend to run for it.

Mar. What! Were you not sincere in accepting the position of Dunmore's doctor?

Fan. Not a bit of it. That was merely diplomacy. When you are in the devil's grip, tickle his palm if you want to get

10

out of it. I accepted the position, but I will discharge myself at a convenient time. And now to see how the land lays with the view to skipping. [*To* Dunmore: Captain, this place seems well adapted to your purposes.

Dun. A better place could not be found on the whole Atlantic coast. It is one my old uncle Tom found out when he was engaged in the trade. When he died I got hold of it. Secret and landlocked, and the entrance to the lagoon known only to me, I could turn a thousand negroes loose here and not one of them could get away.

Enter Jones, *followed by the crew. They range themselves on one side, facing* Dunmore *and* Jones.

Dun., (*to crew*). Now, men, I've got a word to say to you before we sail. I suppose you all know what sort of a craft the Sea Hawk is. She is a slaver, and if any of you haven't found it out it is too late to do so now. That's the long and the short of it. Before we sail I'm going to give you all a frolic ashore. You shall have all you can eat and plenty of grog. Now you can look around and see what the place is like. But I warn you all, and every man that hears my voice, to keep away from that grove yonder, where you see that cabin. Don't go within twenty rods of it, or you will get a bullet through you. That's all I've got to say. Now disperse and get ready for a high old time tomorrow.

[*Crew disperse, seemingly elated.* Carson *walks back.* Dunmore *and* Jones, *engaged in conversation, walk to a tree, behind which* Fanshawe *places himself unobserved and listens.*

Dun., (*to Jones*). Now, you can go and relieve Short, who is on guard at the cabin there. You will have to take the duty between you, for there is no one else I can trust. The girls mustn't be discovered. They must be taken over pure or the dealers on the coast won't have 'em. I can get a thousand niggers for one of the girls over there. When we get ready to sail we must get 'em on board secretly at night, and they must be kept out of sight for the entire voyage. We have done the same thing before, and I reckon we can do it again.

Jones. Easily, Captain. It was often done by your uncle, with my assistance, and no one else on board any the wiser.

Dun. Good. There is one of the girls that must be kept mighty close. If she should get out, hell would be to pay here. Now go and relieve Short at the cabin. I will keep you provisioned.

[*Exit* JONES. DUNMORE *retires back.* FANSHAWE *comes from behind the tree.*

Fan. Well, it was certainly very-kind of Captain Dunmore to let me overhear that conversation. Now I understand what his mysterious cargo is composed of. He has got some girls in that cabin—white slave girls, doubtless—that he intends to take over to the coast and exchange for wild negroes. Verily, Captain Dunmore is a slave-trader somewhat in advance of his age. But why should hell be raised here if one of them should be discovered? Good God! can it be possible? A dark suspicion enters my mind, and now I will have a look into that cabin. George! [MARLOWE *approaches.*] Come, get ready to follow me. I am going to see what that cabin contains.

Mar. Don't attempt it, Dick. You heard Dunmore's commands to his crew. They were intended for us as well.

Fan. Nevertheless I am going to have a look into that cabin, if I risk my life in getting it.

Mar. But why are you so determined on that?

Fan. That will be explained before the door of the cabin— and perhaps the explanation will walk out of it. Come, we will take some guns and pretend to be going after game. I see that by making a detour we can get into the rear of the grove without being seen from here. [*To* DUNMORE: Captain, I've a notion that game must be plentiful around here.

Dun. There is no end of it. This is a regular hunter's paradise.

Fan. Well, shooting is a sport that Marlowe and I delight in ; so if you will let us have some guns we will see what we can find for an hour or so.

Dun. There are guns enough—those breech-loading 'rifles against the tree and some muskets on the dock.

Fan. We will take the rifles.

Dun. Cartridges you will find in that box there at the foot of the tree. But the rifles are loaded. Empty guns with so much liquor around won't do for the crew I've shipped.

[FANSHAWE *and* MARLOWE *take rifles.*

Dun. Return in time for breakfast. It will be served at 12.

Fan. Well, as no true sportsman would leave the hunt for breakfast, suppose we take some lunch along.

Dun. Very good. I'll send Uncle Dan after you with some. Uncle Dan, go to the cook and have him put up some lunch for the hunters. At same time have some put up for Mr. Jones at the cabin. Take it to him; and then follow after the doctor.

Old Dan. Yes, mars'.   [*Exit.*

                 [*Exeunt* FANSHAWE *and* MARLOWE.

SCENE II—*The grove of oaks and palmettoes. On left a negro cabin, with windows boarded up.* JONES *is seated at a small table beside the door, dozing. A gun, with bayonet attached, is leaning beside the cabin.*

Enter OLD DAN, *carrying two small baskets. Goes to the cabin and sets one of the baskets on the table before* JONES.

Old Dan. Dar be some lunch for you, sah, dat de mars' Cap'n bid me bring you.

Jones. All right, uncle. [*Opens basket and looks in, then shuts it with an indignant slam.*] The Captain seems damnably afraid I'll have a little liquor.

Old Dan. P'raps he know better dan to give it to you, sah.

                      [*Walking away.*

Jones. What's that you say, you grinning old baboon? Hyar! [*Throwing toward him a tin cup which he takes from the basket.*] Bring me some water from the spring, and be quick about it.

Dan., (*picking up the cup*). Yes, sah.

Jones. What have you got in that other basket?

Old Dan. Some lunch for de doctor an' de oder man.

Jones. Let me look at it.

Old Dan. No, sah.

Jones. Bring it hyar, I say.

Old Dan. No, sah.   [*Exit, R.*

Enter FANSHAWE *and* MARLOWE, *R. They stand behind a tree, where they can see* JONES, *but are unseen by him.*

Mar. What a weird and spooky spot! so secret and so mysterious! What in the world can Dunmore have in that cabin that requires such precaution?

Fan. Something that all his precaution will not prevent being discovered. And it is going to be done here and now. Now, don't start or make any outcry when I tell you that Rose Vaughn is in that cabin.

Mar. Good God, Dick! How can it be possible? How in the world could she get there?

Fan. It is easily accounted for. Call to mind where it was that Rose disappeared. It was in a wild region close upon the Florida border. Between that region and his rendezvous here there must be some connection—some route by which he runs his wild Africans into the upper slave States. Then how easy would it have been for Dunmore, instead of conducting Rose to Miss Dunmore's plantation, as he was pretending to do, to bring her forcibly along that route to this spot?

Mar. Oh, Dick, you distress me beyond measure! But for what object can Dunmore have done this?

Fan. For an object that fairly chills my blood with horror. He intends to take her to the African coast and sell her there for a slave. I overheard him confess as much to the old devil who sits over there.

Mar. Good God! could Dunmore do anything so horrible?

Fan. Could he do it? Why, he could put his sister on the block had she been born to a slave's condition. Dunmore would have two objects in carrying out this design against Rose. One would be to wreak vengeance upon her for some wrong that he claims she has done him, and for which he hates her intensely; the other, to get possession of her estate, of which he claims to have been defrauded.

Mar. But this design shall not succeed. No; not if I must sacrifice my life in an attempt to prevent it—not if I have to kill Dunmore in his tracks. But can we not rescue her? Is there no way to do it?

Fan. There may be. But first, let us be certain that Rose is in that cabin. There is just a bare possibility that I am deceiving myself. And now for a scheme to find out the truth. I will work my way up to old Mephisto there, and contrive to stumble against the cabin door and force it open. Then a look within may be had. Come!

[*They leave the tree and come out to the view of* JONES.

Jones. Ah, Doctor, is that you? I hardly expected to see you here. You know this is forbidden ground.

Fan.   It is not forbidden to us, Mr. Jones. We were passing the spot on the lookout for game, so I thought I would step in and get a few details for that life of yours that I intend to write.

                    [*Approaching the cabin.*

Jones.   I can't tell you anything here, Doctor. It may be all right for you, but it would be as much as my life is worth if the Captain found it out.

Fan.   Well, then, we will wait until a more fitting opportunity.   [*Walking back.*

            Re-enter OLD DAN.   *He takes water to* JONES.

Fan., (*to Marlowe*).   So, that scheme fails. Now I am going to see if something can't be got out of the old darkey here. He goes about as if he had some weight on his mind, and I've a notion that it relates to that cabin. Uncle Dan!

Dan.   Yes, mars' doctor.   [*Comes forward.*

Fan.   You have got our lunch there, have you? Well, let us see what it is. [*Takes basket and opens it.*] Sandwiches and oranges, a bundle of cigars, and a bottle of brandy. I wish the Captain had sent claret instead of brandy.

Dan.   Dere was no claret handy, sah. Mars' Captain say he t'ink you worry along on de brandy.

Fan.   We will make it do. Would you like a glass of brandy, uncle?

Dan.   Dat I would, sah.

      [FANSHAWE *takes bottle and cup from basket, pours out a drink,*
            and gives it to OLD DAN. JONES *seems agitated.*

Dan.   'Tank you kindly, sah.   [*Drinking.*

Fan.   Now, uncle, can you bring us some water from the spring?

Dan.   Yes, sah.   [*Takes cups and exit.*

Fan.   Now, when the old fellow comes back I will question him as to Dunmore's movements during the past four months and see if I can trace him from Alabama to this place within that time.

            Re-enter DAN, *with water.*

Fan.   Thanks, uncle. How long have you lived here, uncle?

Dan.   About seben year, sah.

Fan.   Taking care of the place while your master was away, I suppose?

Dan. Yes, sah.

Fan. You were here, then, about four months ago, when your master came down from Alabama?

Dan. Yes, sah.

Fan. Did he come alone?

Dan. No, sah. He bring a young lady wid him an' an octoroon girl.

Fan. So! A young lady, eh, and an octoroon girl! Was the young lady a handsome, dark-eyed lady?

Dan. Dat she was, sah.

Fan. The octoroon girl was a slave, wasn't she?

Dan. She was, sah.

Fan. Well, uncle, what did your master do after he brought the young lady here?

Dan. He go away for about two months, sah.

Fan. And last night he came back on the schooner?

Dan. Yes, sah.

Fan. And what did he do last night when he came ashore alone?

Dan. I can't tell you nothin' 'bout dat, sah. Mars' Dunmore forbid me to talk, an' he kill me for shuah if he 'spicion dat I say a word.

Fan. Oh, you need not tell me, uncle. I know what he did. He took the young lady and the octoroon girl out of the house and shut them up in that cabin.

Dan. Lord, sir, how you find dat out? Dat was 'zactly what he do.

Fan. Did the young lady have anything to say?

Dan. Yes, sah. Dere was an awful time, sah. She talk to Mars' Captain powerful hard. Den he read to her some papers dat he hab, which make her out to be his slave. Den she quiet down and say no mo', an' den he take her an' de oder girl an' shut 'em up in de cabin dere.

Fan. His slave? What can that mean? Did the young lady look like a slave, uncle?

Dan. No, sah. Dough she might ha' been one. Plenty o' slave girls in de Souf, sah, dat be well raised.

Fan. His slave? The mystery deepens.

Mar. We may be deceiving ourselves, Dick. She may indeed be some handsome, well-reared slave that has come into Dunmore's possession. There are thousands of such girls in the Southern States.

Fan. Well, the mystery is going to be solved before we leave this spot. Now, uncle, you can go to the spring for water, and wait there until we come to you.

Dan. Yes, sah.   [*Takes cup and exit.*

Fan. Now for the key that shall unlock the mystery of that cabin. [*Takes bottle from basket.*] And one that Dunmore has himself placed in my hands—this bottle of brandy. I have discovered that old Jones's weakness is liquor. I will leave this bottle exposed on the fallen tree so that he can see it, and then we will walk off as if going to the spring for water. Instead of doing that we will place ourselves out of view of Jones, and we shall see the old devil walk right into the trap set for him. Now, take a sandwich and a cup and go off as if going to the spring. I will call to you, but don't answer, and I will soon join you.

[MARLOWE *takes sandwich and a cup and goes out.* FANSHAWE *then takes bottle, pours liquor into a cup, then puts bottle back into the basket, with the neck projecting over the side, and sets it upon the fallen tree.*

Fan., (calling). Ho, George! is that old darkey ever coming with that water? I can't drink this brandy without some. Ho, uncle! H'm! I must go after him.

[*Takes sandwich and cup and exit.* JONES *rises from chair, looks cautiously around, then crouches and creeps to basket, lifts out bottle, and takes several pulls at it. Replacing bottle, he creeps back to cabin and lays himself across the threshold of the door.*

Re-enter FANSHAWE, MARLOWE, *and* OLD DAN.

Fan. The cunning old devil! Foreseeing that he would be drunk, he has laid himself squarely across the threshold of the door, so that it will be impossible to get into the cabin without passing over his body.

Mar. Will you try to enter?

Fan. No, it would be too hazardous. Nothing must be risked now. I will try another plan, one that my novel-writing fancy has put me up to. Now go and stand under the cabin window and sing a verse of some song. If Rose is there she will recognize your voice and may answer.

Mar. Fortunately, I know a song that I have often heard her sing.

[MARLOWE *goes to the cabin, stands under the boarded window and sings in a low voice,* "Oh, sad were the moments when my love and I parted," *then listens with his ear to the window. There is no response. He then taps softly on the boards, sings another verse, and again listens, but no answer is returned. The cabin door is slightly opened, but* JONES *stirs uneasily and it is quickly closed.* MARLOWE *comes forward.*

Fan. No answer! Can it be possible that we are deceiving ourselves after all?

Mar. I cannot think so. And the thought that she may be there is too maddening. I cannot endure the suspense, and I will know. [*Starts toward cabin.* FANSHAWE *grasps him.*

Fan. Stop! You will only bring destruction upon yourself and make certain her fate if she is there. Wait and trust to me—to my chance of drugging Dunmore and his crew tomorrow. Everything depends upon that. Now let us go back and await events.

[FANSHAWE *and* MARLOWE *take rifles and exeunt.* OLD DAN *follows with baskets.*

SCENE III—*Same as Scene I in Act V. A table under the trees on left, at which* DUNMORE *and* CARSON *are seated playing cards.* MISS DENHAM *seated apart reading.* JUDGE CROTCHET *walking moodily up and down. Several of the crew lounging about.*

Enter FANSHAWE, MARLOWE, *and* OLD DAN.

Dun. Hello! here come the hunters, and without game. How is this, Dick? Couldn't you find anything to shoot?

Fan. No, nothing worth shooting at. And we found ourselves in no mood for shooting, anyhow. The languid influence of the clime, the etherial sunshine, and odor-laden air, took the murderous impulse out of us, and so we sat ourselves down under a tree to chat and smoke and listen to the far-off roar of the surf. And so the time slipped away until it was too late to do any hunting, and we come back. But we got on the track of some game, however, that we hope to bag tomorrow. If we don't do so you can make game of us, and probably will.

Dun. Well, I am sorry I can't offer you some breakfast. It's over, and the cook is on another of his periodical drunks; but you are in time for coffee and a cigar.

11

[FANSHAWE *and* MARLOWE *place their rifles against the tree, then sit down at table. As they do so there is some commotion outside the scene, and a woman's voice is heard exclaiming, "Let me go, you devil! let me go! I will see him!" Then* ROSE VAUGHN, *with disheveled hair and in a torn and dirty dress, rushes in and stands gazing round in a dazed way. All rise in consternation.* JONES *staggers in, grasps* ROSE *by the wrist, and with the words,* "Hyar, you she devil, come back!" *attempts to drag her off. At this* MISS D. *and the* JUDGE, *recovering from their surprise, start toward* ROSE. *The* JUDGE *thrusts* JONES *aside.* ROSE, *with a hysterical cry, throws herself into* MISS D.'s *arms. The* JUDGE *turns and confronts* DUNMORE.

Miss D. Rose! Rose Vaughn! In God's name, what do you here? Have you dropped from the clouds?

Dun., (*advancing to* JONES *and taking him by the throat*). You drunken, miserable, slush-eating swab! How did that girl get out of that cabin?

Jones, (*crouching*). I got asleep in the doorway, Captain, and the cunning she devil crawled over me.

Dun. Got asleep, did you! [*Raising his fist.*] I have a great mind to brain you here on the spot! Stand up! [JONES *rises.*] You shall have sleep enough. Tomorrow you will swing to an oozy bed in the bottom of the lagoon. Now, go aboard and get ready for it, for by God you shall take it.

[*Gives* JONES *a push that sends him reeling off the scene.* DUNMORE *then walks to table, against which he leans with folded arms, and defiantly waits what is to follow.* CARSON *walks aside.*

Fan., (*to Marlowe*). So! She was there! Now, George, control yourself. Don't look at Rose or utter a word. We must make no mistake now or everything is lost.

Mar. Don't fear for me, Dick. I shall control myself, if it is only for the purpose of killing John Dunmore, if Rose cannot be saved. [*A slight pause.*

Dun. Well, ladies and gentlemen!

Judge, (*advancing to* DUNMORE). Now, John Dunmore, what is the meaning of this? Why is that lady here?

Dun. She is here because she has escaped from the place where I saw fit to confine her. She is my slave, Judge, if that makes my meaning any clearer.

Judge. Your slave! John Dunmore, if you say that girl is your slave you lie to the depths of your malignant heart.

Miss D. My God! What does this mean? This girl a slave!

Dun. Yes, Miss Denham, my slave. She was born in a negro cabin—born her father's slave—and when he died I got hold of my property the best way I could.

Judge. No, Miss Denham, she is no more his slave than you are. Born in a negro cabin she was, but not born her father's slave. That was a story put forward to cover a family disgrace. Well he knows who her mother was, and well I know it. As her father's lawyer, I was made acquainted with all the details of that sad history.

Dun. I don't care what you have been told or what you say. I say that she is my slave, and I say that I can prove it.

Judge. I say that you cannot prove it.

Dun. I can, and I will do it here. Here are the proofs. Examine them for yourself, and disprove them if you can.

[*Takes papers from his coat and throws them upon the table.*

Judge. I will examine them—and you shall see how easily I will tear in pieces your pretended proof and expose the mesh of fraud and perjury by which you have ensnared and seek to make your slave the daughter of your kinsman and benefactor.

Dun. Do so! (*Sneeringly.*)

[JUDGE *takes up papers and looks them over. While he does so the crew, attracted by the scene, come in and gather in a group at back near the veranda.*

Judge, (*throwing papers upon table*). Pah! Just what I expected to find—a flimsy chain of fraud and perjury, contrived with the design of wreaking revenge upon that girl and getting her estate under cover of the forms of law. But you will fail, Dunmore. Your pretended proof is not worth the paper it is written on.

Dun. Don't be quite so certain of that, old man. They are enough to satisfy the law, and that is enough to satisfy me.

Judge. They are not enough to satisfy the law. The law has been cheated—outraged. Who was the judge whose name is signed to these papers? One of your own kindred—one who knew he was putting the stamp of legality upon fraud in order to avenge upon this girl a wrong done by her father and for which he had done his best to atone.

Dun. It is easy enough to say all this. What proof have you got of it?

Judge. I have proof that will overwhelm you. Let us go back to the time when, in the confusion following her father's death, you sneaked away to his safe, tore the signature from his will, and stole the certificate of his marriage to Rose's mother. You got the original certificate, I admit, but you left behind you a copy of it, which was engrafted in a legal document, duly witnessed and sworn to and as valid in law as the original itself. In your nervous haste it was dropped from the other papers, and there, under a corner of the safe, it was found by me on the very day you left the house.

Dun., (apparently off his guard). That paper was a fraud. The man who performed that marriage ceremony was a fraud. He was a cross-roads justice, whose time had run out and who was not re-elected.

Judge. Not so fast, my friend. No one was elected in his place, and his act was afterward declared legal by the highest court of the State. Her father took good care to guard the rights of his daughter against enemies that he knew, in case of his death, would rise up against her. · So you are baffled there, and you are baffled everywhere. I saw through your design the day I found the paper you had left behind you, and that very day I caused Rose to make a will by which, in case of her death, her property would go to other relatives. And there stands one who witnessed that will, and who can prove what I say. ·   [*Pointing to* Miss Denham.

Dun. Miss Denham, is this true?

Miss D. It is true.

Dun. Then the fate of that girl is sealed. I would go on now in what I have undertaken if the very devil bade me stop. [*To the* Judge: You talk to me of my revenge. Have I nothing to avenge on the woman who prevented my marriage to a lady who would have been my wife? Who deprived me of a chance of fortune that her father held out to me, and who drove me to become a beggarly clerk in your office, and who wills away from me an estate which in justice should be mine, and of which I was robbed by a wrong done to my family—a wrong so deep that my own mother made me swear to avenge it. The time to avenge that wrong has come, and by heaven I will not let it pass.

Judge. Dunmore, you know that in opposing your marriage to her cousin, Rose was but doing her duty. But enough of this. You are master here and your will is law. Let us know for what purpose you have brought Rose here, and the nature of the revenge you intend to inflict. [DUNMORE *does not answer.*] Come, speak, man.

Rose. He will not tell you. He dare not. I will tell you. By a forged letter he lured me into his power. By lies and treachery and violence he has brought me here, where he holds me for a fate worse than death itself. He intends to take me to the African coast and sell me there as a slave.

Judge. That he shall never do.

Miss D. My God! Can this be true? No, no. I cannot believe it. [*Advancing to* DUNMORE.] Captain Dunmore, why do you not speak? Does she speak the truth?

Dun. Miss Denham, I intend to dispose of my own property to my best advantage. [*Turns away.*

Miss D. My God! Can it be possible that this man can enact such villainy? Ah, now I see it all! I, too, have been tricked and betrayed. Mr. Carson, have you nothing to say? Are you a confederate in this plot against this girl?

Car. No, Miss Denham. I—have—had nothing to do with this. [*Aside:* I dare not tell her the truth.

Miss D. Ah, thank God, that you can say this! And now let us save Rose. It is in your power to do so. Oh, look back to the beginning of this dreadful business! See in it the direct result of your crime and my crime against her. Oh, now let us make some reparation for that crime! Oh, save her! Save yourself! Save me!

Car. Miss Denham, I would save Rose if it were in my power. Nothing that I can say or do would have the least effect with Captain Dunmore. And let me remind you of something that you seem to overlook. Do you not see that with Rose out of the way a great obstacle to your happiness is removed?

Miss D. What! Do you say this to me? You! Can it be possible that you have fallen so low—that you can think so meanly of me as to believe that I would again yield to that temptation? No! and to redeem myself from the guilt and the shame that it has brought upon me I would shed my heart's blood upon this spot. And if you have tricked and betrayed

me into a participation in the plot against this girl I would shed
yours with as little remorse as I would crush a viper under my
feet.

> [CARSON *turns away and joins* DUNMORE. *They walk aside and
> confer. As they do so there is some movement among the
> crew. One of them, who stands near the baskets of brandy
> on the veranda, lifts up the tarpaulin covering them and
> looks in. Then, looking cautiously around and seeing that
> he is unobserved, he takes out a bottle and passes it to one of
> the crew standing by his side, who quickly conceals it in his
> clothing. He then takes out other bottles and passes them
> along the line until each of the crew has one concealed in his
> clothing. He then covers the baskets. The crew stand for a
> moment as if trying to appear unconcerned, but a panicky
> feeling seems to spread among them, and they make a hur-
> ried exit. During this action on the part of the crew* MISS
> DENHAM *has been walking thoughtfully up and down.*

Miss D. [*Aside:* Yes; I will make the sacrifice. It may save
Rose. Better a life-long expiation as the wife of this man than
to have upon my soul the burden of such a crime as this. [*Approaches* DUNMORE.] Captain Dunmore, will you let me have a
word with you apart? [*They step aside.*] Captain, you have
asked me to be your wife. Your proposal—I—saw fit to decline ;
but if I were now to alter my mind, would you, after what has
passed, renew your proposal?

Dun. I would, Miss Denham, with all my heart.

Miss D. Then I withdraw my refusal to marry you. But you
must grant me one request. You must give up this design against
Rose. It is not alone for her sake or mine that I ask it from
you. It is for your sake as well. If you persist in this work
the day will come when the thoughts of it will rise up in judg-
ment against you. Conscience will awake, and you will curse
the day you were born. It will drive peace from your home,
sleep from your pillow, and end in driving you to madness and
death. So sure as you live this day, so sure will be your fate if
you go on in this work. Vengeance is mine, saith the Lord, I
will repay. Oh, for the sake of your eternal peace, give it up !
Destroy those papers. Set Rose free, and—call me your wife.

Dun. Miss Denham, so great is my desire to call you my
wife that I would make almost any sacrifice to possess you, and

I will say that if I were alone in this business I would set Rose free. But I am not alone.

Miss D. Then God's vengeance fall upon you all—as it surely will! But one thing tell me, Captain. Is Mr. Carson a confederate with you in this design against Rose? He says that he is not.

Dun. He says so, does he? Then I say he is as deep in it as anybody else. [*Turns away and joins* CARSON.

Miss D., (*looking at* CARSON). Oh, the villain! The cursed villain! The hypocrite! The liar! I will kill him! I will kill him! Oh, angels in heaven, must this horrid work go on? Is there no way to save this girl? Oh, Mr. Fanshawe! George! Can you do nothing?

Fan., (*spoken so as to be overheard by* DUNMORE). It would be of no use, Miss Denham. Rose knows that we would save her if we could. But it is impossible. Therefore the least said the soonest mended.

Miss D. Oh, she is lost! She is lost! [*Returning to* ROSE.] Oh, Rose, Rose! we cannot save you. Your tyrant will not relent.

Rose. Plead not with him. As well plead with devils in hell. Leave me to my fate. It cannot be averted. George—Cousin Richard—farewell! We shall never meet again!

Mar., (*stepping from behind the concealment of a tree and taking* ROSE *in his arms as she passes*). No, no, Rose, my dear one, it is not farewell. We shall meet once more. An attempt will be made to save you. If we fail, you shall not be unrevenged. I will kill John Dunmore, and we will die here together. Now go back, and wait and pray and watch. [*Exit* ROSE.

[*As* ROSE *goes out the* JUDGE *sits down and buries his face in his hands.* MISS DENHAM *walks thoughtfully up and down.* CARSON *goes to table, takes up bottle, and finding it empty, goes to baskets on veranda, lifts up tarpaulin covering them, and finding the liquor taken, returns to* DUNMORE, *who is walking moodily about.* MISS D. *pauses and secretly takes knife from table.*

Car. Jack, the crew have carried off your brandy.

Dun., (*distrait*). What?

Car. The crew have got away with the brandy. There isn't a bottle left.

Dun. What! Carried off the liquor? Then they shall give it back or I'll kill a dozen of them.   [*Takes one of the rifles.*

Car. You will find yourself a little too late, I'm thinking. Your crew will be as drunk as tinkers by the time you reach them.

[*Exit* DUNMORE *hurriedly in the direction of the lagoon.* MISS DENHAM, *in passing, stops near the rifles and overhears the remark of* CARSON. *In a seemingly half-dazed way she gives attention to what he is saying.* CARSON *walks away.*

Miss D. Oh, my prayer is answered. This thought is inspiration. These weapons! We may save Rose.

[*Keeping her look fixed upon* CARSON, *she cautiously hurries to* FANSHAWE *and* MARLOWE. FANSHAWE, *with his back turned toward her, is leaning despondingly against a tree.*

Miss D., (*cautiously*). Mr. Fanshawe! George! Our chance has come! We may save Rose—and save ourselves.

Fan., (*despairingly*). There is no chance to save her. She is lost—and we are lost.

Miss D., (*speaking hurriedly*). She is not lost! For God's sake, listen to me! Our enemies have delivered themselves into our hands! The crew have carried off the liquor and are drunk and beyond the power of resistance. Do you not see what you can do with these rifles in your hands? Seize them! Shoot that devil dead where he stands! [*Pointing to* CARSON.] Dunmore and his crew will then be at your mercy—and we can save Rose —save ourselves!

Fan. By the gods, you are right! There is a chance indeed— if the crew are drunk. But of that we must be certain. [*A shot is heard outside the scene.*] George, see what that shot means.

[*Takes rifle and examines it.*

Mar., (*standing among the trees at back*). The crew are not drunk. Dunmore has them corralled on the wharf, and is parleying with them.

Miss D. But this does not defeat us! Is there no chance — no hope?

Fan. Yes, Miss Denham, there is a chance; but it is a most desperate one. With the crew sober, we shall have at least twenty to fight, and we are but three.

Miss D. We are four to fight, sir. [*Showing knife.*] Give me but the opportunity to use this weapon, and you shall see how

I will do it. I am no coward, sir. Oh, Mr. Fanshawe! George! let us make the attempt! Heaven will send us aid.

Mar. For God's sake, Dick, let us try it. It is our only chance now.

Fan. Oh, I am agreed. It is a fight that I want—a fight to the death—and such it will be. But, Miss Denham, are you certain that you realize the consequences that will almost certainly follow—the fate that will await you women? The most that we can hope for is to kill Dunmore and Carson. That we shall surely do. Then, our ammunition exhausted, for there is little of it, the crew will rush upon us with their knives and we shall be slaughtered in our tracks. What will then await you women? Do you understand me?

Miss D. I do. It is a fate that we will escape in death. We will fight by your side, and if overcome, we will not survive you.

Fan. You are a brave woman—and a noble woman. And now to the work before us.

[FANSHAWE *and* MARLOWE *take rifles and stand looking at* CARSON, *who is walking thoughtfully about.*

Fan. George, this is your shot.

Mar. No; I cannot shoot him in cold blood. Let him go and take his death in the fight that is to come.

Fan. He must be got off the scene. [*To* CARSON: John, Dunmore is having some trouble with his crew. He may need help.

Car., (*looking up*). True; he may. [*Exit toward the lagoon.*

Mar., (*taking position among the trees*). Be ready, Dick, Dunmore, with some of the crew, are coming up the slope.

Fan., (*taking position with* MARLOWE). Let them come. One of them comes to his death if my aim proves true. Wait! A little closer. And now, John Dunmore, God have mercy on your soul. [*Aims and fires.* MARLOWE *fires.*

Fan. Good shot! He is down!

[*Steps back to rifles, examines and loads them.*

Mar. No! Dunmore is up again. He is only wounded. Now the crew are rushing back to the wharf, taking Dunmore with them.

Fan. The devil must guard him. He moved his head just as I fired.

12

The Judge, (*who is aroused by the firing*).   Dick, what does this mean?

Fan.   It means vengeance, for one thing, Judge, and a possible escape, with the chances a thousand to one against us; but vengeance anyway.

Judge.   Then I am with you in that if it takes me to the gates of hell itself. Give me a rifle, and give me a sight of that damned scoundrel——

[*Takes rifle and places himself beside* MARLOWE.

Fan.   We must be certain that these guns not fail us. [*To* MARLOWE: What are the devils doing now?

Mar.   They are loading the muskets on the wharf. Dunmore is binding his head with a handkerchief. He don't seem to be much hurt by your shot. Now he commences to harangue his crew, and is pointing this way. Now they have started up the slope toward us.

Fan., (*joining the* JUDGE *and* MARLOWE). And now the battle begins. Now they are within range! Let them have it.

[FANSHAWE, MARLOWE, *and the* JUDGE *fire. There are return shots, and then a pause. At this moment three sailors appear upon the scene in rear of* FANSHAWE *and* MARLOWE.

First Sailor.   Ahoy, doctor!

Fan., (*turning and meeting them*).   What! Hiram, Jackson, Maloney! Have you come to help us?

First Sailor.   We have, doctor. We want to get even with the Captain for shanghaeing us, and we don't like this slave trading. We were getting ready for a run when we heard the firing. We knew what it meant, and got here as quick as we could.

Fan.   Ah, thank God! thank God! Brave men and true sailors! Now we shall win! Does Dunmore know that you are here?

First Sailor   He does not, sir. He is wounded, and has got no more ammunition. But he will attack you, sir. It is his only chance. But I don't think the crew will make much of a fight, sir.

Mar., (*from the trees*).   Dunmore and his crew seem to be getting ready for a rush, Dick. They have left their muskets and are creeping through the bushes this way.

[*The* SAILORS *take rifles, and with* FANSHAWE *place themselves by the side of the* JUDGE *and* MARLOWE.

Fan. Reserve your fire until they are close upon us. Then drop the man in front of you, club your guns and rush in, and we will drive them to the sharks of the lagoon.

Miss D., (*standing apart*). Now the fateful moment comes. A few minutes more and we shall be free or dead. But whatever the end is to be, it shall be the end of you, John Carson. Though I am hacked to pieces, I will live until I have wreaked vengeance upon you.

> [*Takes position apart at a tree. A short pause follows, then with a yell* DUNMORE *and his crew rush to the attack. They are met with a volley. A confused struggle follows, which is indistinctly seen amid the trees.* MISS DENHAM, *with knife drawn, starts forward and engages in the fight. The crew give way and fly.* FANSHAWE *and the others pursue. A few shots are heard in the direction of the lagoon. For a few moments the scene is deserted. Then—*

Enter CARSON, *as if in flight. He is stripped of coat and vest and on his shirt are marks of blood. He staggers to a tree.*

Carson. Ah, it is all over! The cowards made no fight at all. [*Leans heavily against the tree and lets fall his knife.*] Ah, that fury of a woman! I may yet get away.

> [*Starts forward. As he does so—*

Enter MISS DENHAM, *with hair disheveled and in disordered dress, on which are marks of blood. With knife in hand, she confronts* CARSON.

Miss D. No, John Carson, do not think to escape from me. Here you are to end your miserable life.

Car., (*putting out his hand*). Stop! Your work is done. Give me—a—few moments' life. I have—something to say——

Miss D. Ask no mercy at my hands—from the woman whose life you have ruined! Die, coward and hypocrite! [*Stabs him.*] Betrayer and murderer of your friend! Thief of his daughter's good name! Die! die!

> [*Stabs him successively. With a groan,* CARSON *sinks down.* MISS DENHAM *stands over him.*

Miss D. And so my work is done. He is dead. The end is here. [*Raising aloft her knife.*] Oh, spirits of the dead!—

Doughton!—Herbert Vaughn! Do you look down upon this? Are you avenged?

[*As she stands over the body of* CARSON *enter* FANSHAWE, *with gun in hand, leading* ROSE; MARLOWE. JUDGE CROTCHET, *and* OLD DAN, *who is leading an Octoroon girl, follow.*

Miss D., (*starting forward with an hysterical cry of joy and clasping* ROSE *in her arms*). Oh, Rose! You live! you live! You are free! You are saved! Thank God! thank God!

Mar., (*seeing the blood on Miss D.'s dress*). Aliena, you are hurt!   [*Taking her in his arms.*

Miss D. Yes, George; I am hurt; and hurt to death. [*Laying her head upon his shoulder.*] I have not another hour to live.

Mar. Oh, no, no! Do not say this! Dear girl, you must not die now—in the very moment of victory.

Miss D. Yes, George, my time has come. I must die here!

Mar. Oh, too bad! too bad! Dick, can you do nothing for her?

Miss D. No, dear, he can do nothing for me. I am beyond all earthly hope. No, it is not too bad. It is better that I should die here and now. For so ends the heartache, so ends the long remorse. But my work is not yet complete. I have something still to do.

Mar. What do you mean, Aliena?

Miss D. I mean that I have a work of expiation still to do—some dregs of a bitter cup to drain. [*Turning to the others.*] Now hear me—hear me all—hear the last words of a dying woman, who before she passes to her account would free her soul by an act of reparation to one whom she has greatly wronged. Rose, the man who lies there, and who stole from you your reputation, was not alone in that work. I was confederate with him and aided him in it. I placed him in your bedchamber on that fatal night. It was a plot to separate you from the man you loved. But do not think that it was of my own free will that I joined in the plot against you. I was compelled to do so. I had previously known this man, and he knew of something in my past life which as an honorable woman I could not greatly blame myself for, but which if made known would from the misconstruction that would have been placed upon it have taken from me friends that I dearly loved and destroyed my peace of mind forever. This secret this man threatened to reveal unless I aided him in his design against you. Terrified by his threats and overpersuaded by his arguments, I yielded and did his work. The end of that work is here. There lies the man who stole from you your good name, and here stands the woman who killed him. Oh, Rose, Rose, when you shall think of this hereafter, do not forget the tears I have shed, the remorse I have suffered, for the work of that fearful night. Remember what I have done to avenge you and make a reparation that shall clear your name to the world—and restore you to the man you love. And now, if you can, let me have your forgiveness.

Rose. Forgive you? Yes, yes, noble woman, you have my forgiveness for whatever wrong you have done me! Oh, do not die! but live, live, to be my own loving, dear sister.

Miss D. George, can you forgive me? Do not think too harshly of one who lost her way through this dismal world, who fell before a temptation she could not resist, but who in death redeemed herself.

Mar. Forgive you, Aliena? Yes, yes! You have my forgiveness, and with it my tears—tears that will never cease to fall when I shall think of you. Redeemed yourself! Yes, Aliena, with high, heroic noble sacrifice! And was it not you who saved us all—you who found the way to do so when all hope was lost?

Miss D. Oh, God bless you, George, for these words. They ease the bitterness of parting. [*Leans her head upon* MARLOWE's *shoulder.*] And now, if I have earned the forgiveness of Heaven—I—

[ROSE *and* MARLOWE *seat her upon a bench. She dies.*

Rose. Oh, she is dead! she is dead! Oh, angels, take her to your rest.

[*As they stand with uncovered heads round the body of* MISS DENHAM, *enter the three sailors, bringing in* DUNMORE *bound.* FANSHAWE, MARLOWE, *and the* JUDGE *stand away, and* DUNMORE *is led up to the bodies of* CARSON *and* MISS DENHAM.

Fan. And so, Dunmore, you have come to look upon what your villainy has led to.

Dun. Traitor!

Fan. Call me so, Dunmore. I am proud of such treason.

But you are the traitor, and have earned a traitor's fate. Your treason has recoiled upon your own head.

Dun. H'm! Well, the game is up.

Judge. It is up indeed with you, Dunmore; and has ended as all games end that are played with the devil. He stocks the cards in all games that are played with him. And his stake he will receive at the hands of the hangman, I'm thinking. The law has yet to deal with you, Dunmore.

Dun. I reckon not, Judge.

[Dunmore's *head falls upon his breast, his knees give way, and he sinks down. Sailors ease him to the ground.* Fanshawe *bends over him.*

Rose. Pray for him. His soul is passing away.

Fan., (*rising*). He is dead.

Judge. And so ends the long, dark drama of revenge and hereditary hate. There lies the last victim of the vendetta.

Fanshawe *and the* Three Sailors *come forward.*

Fan. Where did you find the captain?

First Sailor. Lying in the bushes by the lagoon, sir, badly wounded. The mate was lying by him, dead. We thought best to make the captain prisoner and bring him in.

Fan. What has become of the rest of the crew?

First Sailor. Those who were not killed got away in one of the schooner's boats, sir.

Fan. Do you think you can, with the assistance we can give you, take the schooner back to New York?

First Sailor. We can, sir.

Fan. Then we will sail tomorrow.

[*They retire back, and stand uncovered round the bodies of the dead. The sun is setting.*

CURTAIN.

JUDD & DETWEILER, PRINTERS,
WASHINGTON, D. C.